DAVIE'S HEART WAS POUNDING . . .

He had just put the letters in his pocket when he heard footsteps coming slowly up the stairs. He had to hide quickly!

"Did you read about Brauer?" a voice asked.

"Died during lecture."

"Nicely put. Good thing we've got those letters."

"Where are they?"

"In the drawer over the landing."

Davie's heart beat even louder.

"Let me see them." The stranger crossed the room and opened the drawer.

"They're not there."

"What the hell—?"

Davie realized if he stayed where he was, he had one hope in a thousand. The two men were five paces from the door. It was now or never.

He stepped boldly into the light. . . .

Murder Ink.® Mysteries

Scene of the Crime® Mysteries

A Murder Ink.® Mystery

DEATH'S
BRIGHT DART

V. C. Clinton-Baddeley

A DELL BOOK

Published by
Dell Publishing Co., Inc.
1 Dag Hammarskjold Plaza
New York, New York 10017

Death's Bright Dart is a quotation from "The Ballad of
Billy of Nosey Bent or How to Make a Poet"
by Charles Causley.
Salads of lilies and ballads of wine, a line quoted in the
course of the story, also comes from this poem.

Dell ® TM 681510, Dell Publishing Co., Inc.

ISBN: 0-440-11944-8

Reprinted by arrangement with,
William Morrow and Company, Inc.
Printed in the United States of America
First Dell printing—June 1982

For
R.H.

ST. NICHOLAS'S COLLEGE KEY

Staircases: A (first floor, *Bondini* and *Jones-Herbert*); C (first floor, *Junge* and *Vorloff*); D (ground floor, the Conference Office = C.O.); G (ground floor, *Mostyn-Humphries*; first floor, *Brauer*; top floor, *Cowl*); M (ground floor, *Krasner* and *Zinty*; first floor, *Davie*).

Doorways: 1, to Master's Lodge from cloisters; 2, to Combination Room stairs from cloisters; 3, to Hall dais from Combination Room.

C.R. = Combination Room; O.W. = Oriel Window; P = Porter's Lodge; X = Archway between First Court and Baxter's Court; Y = Passage to Hall stairs and cloisters.

(Map drawn by Mark Goullet)

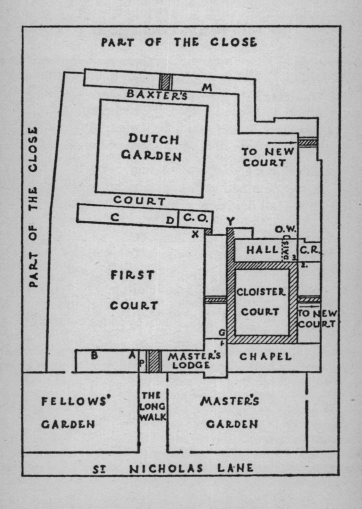

CAMBRIDGE

Friday

I

Dr. Willow entered the Master's garden with caution. During the summer holidays the journey to the Lodge was dangerous. As he passed the first big laurestinus on the right Clarissa, aged six, let fly with two revolvers. Dr. Willow very kindly clapped his hands to his heart and staggered about in agonies. Clarissa went over to the enemy at once. "Richard's behind the rhododendron," she whispered. "He's got an atomic bomb." "Thanks for telling me," said Willow, and proceeded up the path not unmindful of his last encounter with Richard when he had narrowly escaped being holed by an arrow. Richard was seven.

When he reached the rhododendron Willow paused. "Would it be any good if I surrendered?" he asked. "No," said a voice from the other side of the bush. "The mechanism is working. You are domed." "Oh—please," urged Willow, "not domed." To which the voice unexpectedly replied "Bother! It's stuck." "Can I help?" said Willow. "Yes, please," said the voice. So Willow went down on his knees under the rhododendron and presently he and Richard produced a very superior bang and a cloud of red smoke. "Sorry it wasn't ready in time for you," said Richard. "Not at all," said Willow.

Abel, aged five, was behind the next laurestinus, a little put out by the delay at the atomic bomb site. But, being a stoic child, he had stood his ground, and was able to deliver his own assault with considerable success. Willow had forgotten the third hazard and was fairly surprised when a long paper dart, fitted on a mercifully light cane, shot out of the recesses of the bush and hit him in the middle.

"You're dead," said Abel, bustling out of the shadows. "That was a thing like what they have at the Missionary Exhibition, and death is instantaneous."

"Goodness! Where d'you get that word?"

"At the Missionary Exhibition—it's all written on the glass case."

"Let's see who can throw it farthest," said Richard. So for a few minutes all four of them played with the dart until a distant laugh showed that they were providing amusement for five people in the Master's first-floor drawing room. At one of the windows was Dr. Courtney, the Master, with old Dr. Davie and someone Willow did not recognize. At the other was Mrs. Courtney and Catherine, Geoffrey Willow's wife.

"Now children, let Dr. Willow go," called Mrs. Courtney. The Courtney children professed not to hear, but Willow took his opportunity. If he didn't get his tea now he never would. So he hurled the dart with great vigour across a flower bed, and while Clarissa ran round it, and Richard jumped over it, and Abel jumped into it, he gained the sanctuary of Mrs. Courtney's drawing room.

"This is Dr. Willow, our bursar, and secretary for the symposium," said the Master. "Colonel Vorloff."

"How d'you do, sir. Have you found your rooms in college yet?"

"Yes, indeed. They are very good. In the First Court. I look down on roses and red brick. It is lovely."

"Everything ready, Geoffrey?"

"I hope so, Master. It's taken six months to organize this conference—but one never knows till the last minute if anyone's going to come. Our side of the business is all right. We'll see about the rest when they all begin to arrive—in about half an hour that is."

"I was early," said Colonel Vorloff. "I hope not too early. I wanted to see Cambridge, so I came in the morning. I walked round your beautiful Close and then I met the Master in the court, and he very kindly asked me to tea. I have a start on everybody."

"That seems to be your habit," said Dr. Davie. "I've read your books. The number of places our visitor has been the first person to visit is quite extraordinary."

"Except the nastier parts of Somaliland," said the Master. "Colonel Vorloff must allow Willow a precedence there. I expect you know Willow's book about that grisly country."

"Indeed yes, sir. My first field was nearby in Abyssinia. Then later, far away, in Borneo. There is still plenty of room in the world. One soon loses oneself and starts finding other people."

"Exactly," said the Master. "I'm always expecting to hear of someone running into a brontosaurus, finding a new civilization or uncovering a lost one."

Catherine said, "I think it's time I took Geoffrey to the office. I'm going to help check the people in."

"Goodness, yes!" said Willow. "We must go. Thanks for the tea."

"I do hope the children haven't had time to invent anything new," said Mrs. Courtney, whose reliance upon Hope for the successful upbringing of her family had long been a matter of astonishment in Cambridge circles.

"Don't worry about them," said Dr. Davie. "They're good enough children and they have at least one virtue."

"Indeed they have not," said Mrs. Courtney, "not one. It is a great disappointment."

"Come! They are none of them suffering from the distressing delusion that they are express trains."

"That is something to be thankful for, certainly. But no positive good replaces the train. The virtue is negative."

"So many virtues are," said Dr. Courtney.

"I think I ought to depart before we become too involved in defining the Good Life," said Dr. Davie. "Would you care to come with me, Colonel Vorloff? I'd be very happy to show you round the college before we get too crowded."

"I would be most grateful, sir. Goodbye, Master. Goodbye, Mrs. Courtney. Thank you for your very kind reception."

"There they go, the sweet creatures," said Mrs. Courtney. She was standing by the back drawing room window, which looked down upon First Court.

"Who?" said the Master, puffing a pipe in the depths of an armchair. "Davie and Vorloff?"

"No—Geoffrey and Catherine. Both so small and both so clever. They are a perfect pair. Do you think he'll get the professorship, Clive?"

"Not with Brauer in the field."

"Bother Brauer!"

"Brauer has all the attack. Everyone likes Geoffrey and he's just as clever, but he's so easygoing he'd as soon be playing with the children as using his microscope. So they underrate him."

"They must be exceedingly stupid. The truth is, Clive, that Geoffrey's extremely ambitious underneath his playful manner. Though not as ambitious as Catherine is. She'd do anything for him—anything."

"Commit—?"

"Well—I don't know," said Mrs. Courtney coolly, "possibly—why not? She gave up a great career to marry him. She might do something remarkable for him now."

"Heaven help us!" said the Master.

"What a lovely voice it was, Clive."

"Still is, isn't it?"

"If she goes on practicing."

"Of course neither of them may get it," said the Master. "Caldecott has a good chance. He's not pushing but he plays his cards admirably. Old Ravenshaw doesn't retire till next summer. Much may happen before then."

Mrs. Courtney sat down and started to eat a late sandwich. "I rather liked Vorloff," she said. "Is he a refugee? One never knows where one is these days with Central Europeans."

"No, he's a genuine accredited Hungarian. I imagine his government has the sense to see that a man of distinction is a good advertisement."

II

Dr. Davie was guiding Vorloff round the cloisters, after a tour of the chapel.

"The place is unique, you see, because it was once a monastery. The older buildings are therefore grouped in the monastic way—the Refectory, now the Hall, the Dormitory, now the Library, the Abbot's Lodging, now the Master's Lodge, and the Chapel, all squared round the Cloisters. The courts beyond have been built at different periods since, from the seventeenth-century court, the one you're staying in, to the ghastly Victorian additions. Thank heavens we've done better in the twentieth century."

"What happened to the monastery?" asked Vorloff. "The Reformation?"

"Not a bit of it. Our visitor suppressed it in 1472. By that time there were only three monks in residence, and, as there was considerable doubt about the sex of one of them, the excellent bishop thought he would be doing a greater service to God if he turned the place into a college. But this center part looks like a monastery, and feels like one, I think: and I'm happy to say that we still have the ghost of a monk."

"Indeed?"

"Or what the undergraduates say is a ghost. I'll show him to you one night."

"A ghost you can produce when you like? That is incredible."

"Precisely," said Dr. Davie. "Now these stairs lead up to the Combination Room—where we combine before dinner, you know. Here—" and he opened the door with love—"here you are in the eighteenth century at once—these comfortable chairs and the curved tables made to fit round the circle for port and dessert. There's a lot of rather nice wiggery on the walls too."

"That's a splendid fellow there," said Vorloff.

"Our best benefactor, Josiah Brady. He left lots of money for scholarships. And a lot for feasts, which I am glad to say no Royal Commission has been silly enough to question. And several pleasant customs. On his audit night the bursar goes round and presents every guest with a button with the words 'For thine especial safety.' It was in the old man's will. We always do it. I suppose he wanted to make a joke which would raise a laugh for him long after he'd returned to dust. . . . This other door opens straight into Hall—on to the dais. That's where we dine. And where Brauer's going to give his lecture on Monday."

Davie pointed to the oriel window at the end of

the dais. "That's our founder's rebus," he said. "Bishop Allbottel—so on all the old college windows you see these coloured bottles and the motto *Procul austeritas, floreat convivium*. We try to live up to the good man's wishes."

In a picture on the center panel behind the dais the Bishop in full canonicals knelt in prayer—but his eyes were open and he seemed to survey the Hall with some amusement.

"There he is. A nice old boy, I think. It was he who bestowed the name of St. Nicholas on the new foundation—but nothing is ever forgotten in an ancient university and the college also retained its older name of Saint Anastasius and the Magnificent Virgin Edwina."

"That's a bold title."

"But deserved, I assure you."

"I detect a story, sir. Please tell me."

"Edwina was a virtuous Saxon lady who took refuge with the monks of St. Anastasius while being pursued by a ruffian with the improbable name of Egglewulf. When Egglewulf threatened to beat down the monastery walls, the admirable Edwina instructed the brethren to open their gates, and then, by a miraculous device, turned herself into a monk; and with such total success that, although the insensitive Egglewulf caused the most searching examinations to be made, he was forced to return to his Eastern marshes without satisfaction. His retreat being established beyond doubt, the excellent Edwina continued on her virgin way to a neighbouring convent, wherein she speedily acquired a remarkable reputation as a herbalist and, in her lighter moments, as an entertaining prestidigitator. In memory of this splendid woman the monks of St. Anastasius were permitted by the head of their order to incorporate the name of Edwina in their title. There is a picture of her in one of our illuminated manuscripts. She appears to be amusing the nuns by juggling with eggs."

"It would explain a lot," said Colonel Vorloff, "if Edwina had been a young man dressed up as a girl. But I suppose that is too complicated a theory."

"Not merely complicated," said Davie, "but gravely heretical. For saying precisely that an unfortunate cobbler called Simkin was torn in pieces by an infuriated mob in, if I remember rightly, the year 1242. It's all written down in the monastery documents."

From outside the oriel window came the chink of chisel on stone, and a figure moved strangely behind the glass as though suspended in air.

"The window's in splints outside because they're repairing the masonry. Now, if we walk through the Hall and down the stairs we'll be in the cloisters again, just by the turning to your rooms."

At the archway leading to First Court they met Cowl. Davie introduced them. "Your beautiful college, Dr. Cowl," began Vorloff.

"Just plain Mister," said Cowl. "That's good enough for me."

"Forgive me."

"Easily. It's one of my hates. Davie is a real Doctor, so is Willow, but for the rest—the place teems with them. Why a man should be considered learned in philosophy after spending two years dissecting the novels of George Eliot I can't tell you."

"Cowl, I need hardly say, is a pure mathematician," said Davie.

"Excuse me, here comes one of our doctors now," said Cowl. "Good afternoon."

"Nothing's right for Cowl. He keeps on the same staircase as this chap and they don't speak. Cowl says he's an imposter. Other people say he's a great scientist. You can say when you've heard him lecture. Ah, Brauer—may I introduce Colonel Vorloff, one of our visitors. We've just been walking round your cloister."

III

Geoffrey and Catherine were sitting in a room in the corner of First Court, which had been turned into a reception office for the conference. The majority of the visitors had checked in now, but a few would probably arrive on the 6:10.

Through the window they could see Davie and Vorloff chatting with Brauer. Then the three separated, each to his own rooms. Dr. Davie's were in the second court, Baxter's Court, an eighteenth-century building exactly fitted to his mind, and possessing a view over the college Close, the lovely park which, even in a city, could still embower the much blessed College of St. Nicholas.

"How I dislike that man!" said Catherine suddenly.

"Which man?"

"Brauer."

"Why?"

"Oh—he's so big, and so handsome, and so popular."

"That's a bad thing?"

"And he knows it."

"Can't help knowing it."

"He could help showing that he knows it. I don't believe he's as clever as he thinks he is. . . . And he stands in your light."

Geoffrey laughed.

"Ha! Now I understand you. But don't deceive yourself. Brauer is a great man. Nobody knows his microbes better."

St. Nicholas's College stands back from the world, at the end of an open paved corridor called the Long Walk, connecting St. Nicholas Lane with the porter's lodge. Several figures now appeared beneath the towered gateway, and Mr. Jump, Head Porter, emerging from his private cavern, was to be seen waving a stately finger in the direction of the conference office.

"Here they come," said Geoffrey Willow, "the last lot, I should hope. Six—seven—is that right?"

"Eight should be."

"Right. Here it is. And a star entry too. I bet that's Miss Yana Marden, New York. Impressed?"

"I'd like to say 'no,' but I am rather."

The eight were now bearing down on the office. Besides Miss Marden they were presumably Mr. Krasner, and Dr. Zinty, both from America, Dr. Junge from Munich, Signor Angelo Bondini from Naples, Miss Banbury and Miss Eggar from two northern English universities, and Mr. Jones-Herbert, an earnest-looking young man from the far west.

The ladies were sleeping in lodging houses outside the college, and, aware of this, Miss Eggar and Miss Banbury had left their bags at the porter's lodge for delivery later. But Miss Marden was already enjoying the services of a porter in the person of Mr. Krasner, and he had brought her cases as far as the office.

"What?" said Miss Marden. "No women sleeping on the campus? You dear old-fashioned things!"

"Your rooms are only just across the road," said Catherine.

"I will come with you," said Mr. Krasner.

Signor Bondini, who had small English at command, cast velvet eyes in the direction of Miss Marden, and offered in a gesture to do as much and more, and Catherine, who was handing out envelopes of instructions, decided in one combined deduction that that one would be the conference's Don Juan, that Mr. Jones-Herbert had probably got wet hands, and that little Dr. Junge, because of his smile, was the nicest of the lot.

Willow noted disapproval in the eyes of Dr. Zinty. "I will take your things to your room, Krasner," he said. "It is next to mine."

"Yes," said Willow, "in Baxter's Court, M staircase. I'll show you."

"Come soon, Krasner," said Zinty.

He stood watching his friend and Miss Marden till they disappeared through the gate-house arch, then turned with a small sigh to Willow. Everyone knew what he meant. As Miss Eggar said to Miss Banbury on their way to their lodgings, "What sort of conference does that young woman think she's attending?" And Miss Banbury laughed because she did not want Miss Eggar to think her slow, but inside herself she thought it was rather to Miss Marden's credit to be so attractive, and after she'd tried the mattress in her bedroom and found it wanting, she fluffed out her gray-brown hair more than she usually did, and chose the frock with roses on it for the cocktail party which the college was giving its visitors on this first evening of the conference.

IV

"Will you come with me, Dr. Zinty," said Geoffrey Willow.

"And Dr. Junge," said Catherine, "you come with

me. Your rooms are only on the next staircase. Signor
Bondini and Mr. Jones-Herbert, if you'll hang on for
two ticks I'll be back."

"What roses!" said Dr. Junge.

"Aren't they lovely against the brick? Here you
are. Only one flight."

The sitting room looked both ways—the front windows into First Court. Catherine led Dr. Junge to
the back windows, which looked out on to Baxter's
Court.

"It's a sort of a Dutch garden," she said. "It's been
there for centuries. One can see it, just like this, in
seventeenth-century prints."

Geoffrey Willow was walking across the court with
Dr. Zinty. Catherine and Dr. Junge watched them
enter M staircase.

"That's all right," said Catherine. "He's safely de-
livered. Now I must get on with my labours, or
Mr. Jones-Herbert and Signor Bondini will get lost.
They're in First Court on the far side. Look—this
pamphlet tells you everything: there's a map and a
timetable. See you presently at the cocktail party.
By the way, your neighbour, across the landing, is
Colonel Vorloff."

Dr. Junge bowed. "That is most interesting," he
said. "I am an admirer. Thank you, Mrs. Willow.
Thank you very much."

Dr. Junge unpacked. Then he walked down and
stood at the open archway of his staircase. Several
delegates were strolling round the neat, small court,
which looked so beautiful, Junge decided, because it
was made of such beautiful materials. Nobody made
bricks that colour nowadays. And nobody made bricks
that small. That was it: the thinness of the rose-red
bricks and the thickness of the mortar. It was entirely simple and supremely dignified.

On the other side of First Court Signor Bondini

was looking out of his window on the staircase next to the great gate. And from his window, on the other side of the same landing, Mr. Jones-Herbert was peering too, but rather more cautiously as though afraid of committing some social solecism. Catherine, who had just escorted them there, was returning across the court to the conference office. On the third side of the court Dr. Brauer stood at his window in the set that was reached from G staircase in Cloister Court. From the window above him Cowl momentarily reviewed the scene. Distantly a figure moved beyond the window of the Master's first-floor drawing room.

The court seemed full of people, the windows full of eyes. Dr. Junge strolled along the flagstone path, past the office, and through the corner archway into Baxter's Court. The Dutch garden was quite empty, and, to his thinking, entirely beautiful. No one else was moving among the clipped yews. No one was watching from the windows. First Court might be famous, but it was Baxter's Court that won Dr. Junge's heart. Slowly he walked across the garden and turned to look back at his rooms from the other side. The back window was framed in yellow roses as the front window had been framed in pink ones. Above the building soared four splendid triangular chimneys.

Then two other figures entered through the archway from First Court. They were Mr. Krasner—his ministry for Miss Marden evidently completed—and Dr. Willow. They walked along the paved way surrounding the garden and disappeared into M staircase. Dr. Junge looked at his watch. There was half an hour before the cocktail party began.

"And that's all the men safely gathered in," said Geoffrey Willow.

"Yes," said Catherine. "I'm just going home to doll

up a bit, and I'll make sure about the last three girls on the way."

"They'll be all right," said Willow. "Mr. Krasner has looked after Miss Marden. Miss Eggar is looking after Miss Banbury. And Miss Eggar is obviously a match for anyone."

V

Dr. Davie was sitting by an open window, looking out on the Close. On the far side of the splendid stretch of grass stood the cricket pavilion with its screen of chestnut trees in the background. Between the trees there were further glimpses of green, for, beyond a protective ditch, St. Nicholas Piece stretched on to the river. Except for Colonel Vorloff visitors to the conference had not yet discovered the open doors inviting them into the Close. The green garden was empty.

Dr. Davie's rooms were on the first floor. From the open window of the set below Davie could hear two men talking.

One said, "Don't make a fool of yourself with that girl, will you."

There was an answer, but Davie missed the words. Then "All right," said the first voice, "but be sensible. And do be clear about this. Once I've done my fingering I don't want you to be seen with me. Keep to yourself. It's essential."

The other voice was clearer now.

"I agree, but I'm still not sure your plan is as easy as you think."

"I didn't say it was easy."

"Well—workable."

"Why not?"

"Opportunity. At any rate I reserve my right to use the alternative plan—"

"We agreed on that."

"Very well. I think perhaps I had better go in."

The voices grew distant, and then a door closed.

Dr. Davie was enchanted. He loved mysteries. What girl? And fingering? That was a gangster word. And what plan? Not after the college plate, surely? Or *was* it "fingering"? It seemed an odd conversation for a couple of conference hounds.

As Davie came downstairs a man emerged from the ground floor set.

"One of our guests, I expect?" said Davie.

"Yes—Zinty, from New York."

"I am Davie, a very ancient Fellow of the college. I live in the rooms above yours, on the first floor. If you are looking for the Oak Room I will be very happy to show you the way—though it's obvious, isn't it?" said Davie, pointing to the many people who were now walking across the court and passing by way of the undercroft into Cloister Court, where a door stood open on a long panelled chamber.

The room was full and Davie stationed himself in the nearest corner. There was plenty to watch—the Master talking with Colonel Vorloff and several other delegates; Catherine endeavouring to conduct a conversation with Mr. Jones-Herbert, who had gone red to the ears in the effort; the tall and handsome Dr. Brauer, surrounded as he usually was by a group of admiring ladies.

On the far side a glamorous young woman was standing in the window embrasure talking to a small dark man of about forty. "The siren, doubtless," thought Davie; "and the friend."

As Zinty made his way towards them the young woman called to him.

"Hi! Zinty! I've got the most wonderful apartment.

The young man that ought to be there's a boxer or something, and he's left the most gorgeous things in his cupboards."

A large man cruised into Davie's corner.

"Watching the sport?"

"Yes, Caldecott, I suppose I am."

"Just look at Cowl staring at Brauer! Fascinated by dislike. Hypnotized by repulsion. And all those infatuated females. How does he do it, Davie?"

"Brauer's reckoned an attractive man, I believe."

"That wasn't what I meant."

"I didn't suppose it was," said Davie enigmatically.

But Brauer had stopped talking to the infatuated females, and was staring across the room in the direction of the glamorous young woman. He seemed to be consulting his memory. Davie followed Brauer's eyes.

"Willow!" said Caldecott, catching at the Bursar's passing sleeve. "Davie wants to know who that charmer is over there."

"I was afraid he would. She's Miss Yana Marden from New York."

"And the men?" said Caldecott.

Davie was glad to have his questions asked for him.

"One's Zinty; the dark one's Krasner, both from New York."

"H'm!" said Caldecott; "they've come a long way for a quiet chat."

"The pleasant-looking chap in the window behind them is Dr. Junge."

"Oh—*that's* Junge," said Caldecott. "I want to meet him."

"And what branch of scientific research has claimed the young woman's attention?" asked Davie.

"Possibly metallurgy," said Caldecott.

"Miss Marden happens to be a perfectly good biologist," said Willow. "It isn't essential to have a face like the back of a cab to be a good scholar."

"No," said Caldecott, "I dare say not. All the same it must dissipate Miss Marden's energies to have the face she's got."

But Miss Marden had finished with Dr. Zinty and Mr. Krasner, at least for the moment. She slipped among the guests, casting kind eyes on Miss Banbury, and merry ones on Miss Eggar, and finally ended up in the Master's circle in an animated conversation with Colonel Vorloff. Krasner followed her with his eyes, but Brauer, Davie noticed, had suddenly lost interest in her. Perhaps, after all, he had been looking at somebody else.

Presently he turned to leave. "Off already?" said Davie, who was still standing near the door.

"Yes, please," said Brauer, "I suppose cocktail parties are a social necessity. But they're death and destruction to me. I can't drink the drinks, and I can't stand the standing."

VI

At dinner the few senior members of the college attending the conference sat at their own high table. By Willow's invitation other places were occupied by visiting lecturers, and the remaining seats were filled by any guest that one of the Fellows happened to ask. Davie asked Zinty, and as they encountered Miss Banbury and Miss Eggar at the door he gallantly invited them too. Davie took the chair at the oriel window end of the long table, Miss Eggar on his right, Miss Banbury on his left. Zinty sat next to Miss Banbury, and Cowl, who had followed them up the Hall, took the seat next to Miss Eggar. At the other end of the

table Brauer was sitting between Willow and Colonel
Vorloff. Krasner, who was one of the last to enter,
found a seat at the far end of the Hall next to Miss
Marden.

"Who was that?" asked Davie, hot on the trail of
his private mystery. "The man who just came in."

"Over there?" said Zinty.

"Yes."

"That is Krasner—from New York. We are old
friends. We were in the same German prison camp.
I am a Czech. He is Hungarian. After the war I
went to America. Krasner went back to Hungary. It
is only since the revolution that we have met again."

"How interesting!" said Davie. "Was he there during the trouble?"

"Yes."

"There was a dreadful book about Hungary published a few years ago," began Miss Banbury—"*Magyar Terror*. I wonder—"

"You can't depend upon that sort of book," said
Miss Eggar. "I have yet to meet anyone who really
knows the true story of Hungary."

"But how do *you* know?" asked Cowl.

Miss Eggar ignored him.

"In reality the revolution was a very small affair,
and even that was incited by American agents. The
mere fact that *Magyar Terror* was published in America anonymously is enough to prove its worthlessness."

"I would not say that," said Cowl. "There are dan-
gers attending outspoken criticism of authoritarian
states."

Zinty bowed across the table. "There are, sir. Mr.
Krasner could tell you. He spent eight years in a
Budapest prison. He had committed great sins. He
was a caricaturist, you see."

"Ah!" said Davie. "The authoritarian state may be
a prime subject for the caricaturist. But the carica-

turist is no subject for the authoritarian state."

"If Mr. Krasner is a caricaturist why does he come to a scientific conference?" demanded Miss Eggar.

"He wanted to be with me. And he is a man who likes to be well informed."

"H'm," said Cowl. "He must be a very respectful follower of the light if he means to absorb an hour's lecture from Brauer without an intimate understanding of what he's talking about. Has he been warned?"

Zinty went slightly pink. "He will find it interesting," he said. "Krasner is a much travelled man. He has been in parts of South America where no white man has ever been before."

"One doesn't have to be a practicing scientist to attend this conference," said Davie. "I'm not a scientist."

"Nor is Colonel Vorloff really. He's a—if I said 'an adventurer' you would misinterpret me."

"Certainly I would," said Cowl. "Instantly."

"But that's what he is, in the best sense. An explorer. A seeker after truth. An adventurer in the jungle. An adventurer in the laboratory. He's himself."

"His books are wonderful," said Miss Banbury. "Especially the animal ones. He has some extraordinary powers of understanding them. Dogs especially."

"There's a splendid book about monkeys too," said Miss Eggar.

Miss Banbury said, "The travel books are rather frightening—the Borneo one particularly. I can never think how explorers take the first step, establish the first confidence. Living with savages must be an art."

"I've lived among savages for twenty years," began Cowl, casting a baleful glance over his shoulder, but Davie added sweetly, "You might suppose, Miss Banbury, that age and crabbed youth could not get on together—but they do."

Some of the crabbed youth were still in residence and were sitting at their own table in a far corner of the Hall.

Baggs, a natural science scholar with undisplined hair, asked "What are they conferring about?"

"Poison, that's what," replied Mostyn-Humphries. "They're going to read papers on 'Barbiturates and the Common Man,' 'The Domestic Uses of Strychnine' and all that. We shall be lucky if we get out of here alive. God! How miraculously ugly that woman is!"

"I think," said Baggs mysteriously, "that they may be fruitful ground."

"Fruitful ground, eh?" said Mostyn-Humphries. "What are you going to do? Stage a one-man sit-down in the court? They'd tear you limb from limb. Particularly that werewolf with the front teeth and the lamentable hairdo."

"I haven't decided what," said Baggs, "but with people here from all over the world I've got to do something."

"Trust you," said Mostyn-Humphries, "and when you've finished cornering the furniture polish, or whatever, I'll be glad if you'll shove it over my way."

At the end of the high table Brauer was deep in conversation with Willow and Vorloff. Before him lay a small flat bottle of tablets which from time to time he spun round with a flick of his finger.

"It was odd enough," he was saying, "that people spent so many centuries conducting serious work in a dead language. But surely it's much stranger that people should still study the classics when in these days they lead one nowhere at all."

"But don't you think people may study the classics for pleasure?" said Vorloff.

"This isn't the age of pleasure," said Brauer, dropping a tablet in his glass of water.

"But surely, doctor—all the more reason for seeking it. You should come with me to the Greek islands. There is peace and pleasure. And absolutely no science."

Brauer drank his medicine.

"I want work," he said. "Fruitful work. Results. That is my pleasure. And I have to work hard to get it. In England there are many rules and inspectors. It is well managed, I agree, but it hampers research. One has to find one's way round some of the restrictions. My dogs have helped me more than some of my colleagues."

Colonel Vorloff's eyebrows contracted. "Your dogs?"

"Are you interested in dogs?"

"Very much."

"Then perhaps you would like to visit my laboratory."

"I should indeed," said Vorloff after a moment's hesitation.

"Then come tomorrow—after the afternoon session."

"Thank you," said Vorloff. "I will do that."

After dinner, on the way back to his rooms, Davie found a group of delegates in Baxter's Court looking up at the ancient brickwork of the Hall.

"A pity it's in splints," he said. "It's a lovely window."

"The one behind you when we were dining?" said Zinty.

"Yes. I don't think one usually sees an oriel so high above the ground—but we go upstairs to our Hall, which isn't usual either. We're repairing the masonry and it's tricky work. There's only one man who knows how to do it, apparently, and the consequence is he's taking his time. He'll have to knock off on Monday when Brauer gives his public lecture.

And it won't be worth coming in just for the morning, and then on Tuesday it will rain. And so it goes on."

One little man asked questions about dates, and how anyone had dared to build the Victorian lecture room which unnaturally divided the Hall from the seventeenth-century First Court.

"It is a terrible thought, Dr. Junge," said Davie, expertly reading the name on the little man's lapel, "but in about a hundred years people may be talking of that building as a nineteenth-century gem." And as they were standing slightly apart he added, "Won't you join Colonel Vorloff in my rooms for a chat and a post-prandial drink?"

"I am sorry, sir," said Junge, "but I have to call on Dr. Brauer. Could you very kindly direct me to his rooms?"

"Certainly—but better than directions is a director. Mostyn-Humphries—"

"Yes, sir?"

"You're going back to your rooms, I don't doubt. Please show Dr. Junge the way to Dr. Brauer's staircase." And Mostyn-Humphries, who kept in the ground floor set underneath Brauer, but was in fact on his way to play bridge with some cronies in St. Nicholas Lane, said that he would, and the two of them turned back under the archway leading to Cloister Court.

VII

Davie brought Vorloff to the windows to admire the Close as it lay wrapped in the July twilight, with a shaving of a moon hanging above the wide empty green.

"Perfect!" said Vorloff. "This is civilization. And so little left. . . . I was talking to Dr. Brauer at dinner."

"Yes. I saw you were."

"He is only interested in his work it seems. Which is very strange."

"Perhaps that's the impression he likes to give. He is not English and he can have no love for our old-fashioned ways. But I see him walking in the Close of an evening—and he looks at peace, and, in his odd barbaric way, happy."

"He's asked me to see his laboratory."

"H'm," said Davie. "You're privileged. He keeps that very much to himself—with the result that, rightly or wrongly, he's the subject of all sorts of remarkable stories."

"Such as—?"

"I don't know that I can go into that. But he's a double-natured sort of man. Gentle in his rare moments of repose. Grateful for the sanctuary that he finds here. But ruthless where his work is concerned I would think. You know the type. Now—what will you have? What, as we facetiously say, is your poison? Whisky? Brandy?"

"Brandy, please."

"You help yourself. Sit here. I'm delighted you came."

"You asked me and I felt you meant it."

"I did. I did. I love talking."

And so they talked for an hour, first about Hungarian universities, and then about Cambridge.

"The great moment," said Davie, "was when the celibacy rule was cancelled. Within a few weeks all the Fellows of this college announced their marriage. The whole lot. I've often wondered how those staid Victorians looked each other in the face without rocking with laughter."

"Perhaps they did," said Vorloff.

"I'd like to think so," said Davie. "But judging from the language of the biographies I hardly believe it."

"Men don't write in quite the same way as they speak and look."

"It's an ideal that they should."

"But only a few achieve that elegance," said Vorloff. "For instance it's only the writer who has time to create a new word."

Davie sipped his brandy.

"We don't create words nowadays as men did when language was in the making," he said. "Slang comes and goes, but how often does a man invent a word like 'aspectabund' for instance? I found it in a late seventeenth-century diary. Think of the pleasure of coining a word like that!"

"And it means?"

"A face abounding in changes of expression—an indiarubber face, someone might say today. But that would be meant as a joke. 'Aspectabund' was a majestic piece of word-making. I shan't be satisfied till I've found an opportunity to use it myself."

"You have long links with the past, Dr. Davie, I can see that."

"Yes—I suppose I do live with too many ghosts."

"Which reminds me, sir—you have excited my curiosity. This college ghost that you can call up at will."

"Oh, that! You can see it on your way back to your rooms."

Vorloff looked at his watch.

"It's half-past ten. I think I should be going back now."

"Then come along. It's early, but I can see you are bursting with speculation."

Davie led Vorloff across Baxter's Court, and then through the undercroft that led to Cloister Court.

"Now," he said, "walk towards the far wall and as you reach the cross path leading into First Court, turn right, but keep your eye on the far wall."

Vorloff did this and returned to Davie.

"Well—did you see our monk?"

"I certainly did."

"He's frightened many people before now."

"And the explanation?"

"Is absurdly simple. Behind you is a light, set rather low. As you walk away from it you cast a long shadow, which you don't notice—but as you reach the point where I told you to turn right the shadow reaches the far wall and climbs up it. You move right. The shadow moves right. And as you disappear it disappears—apparently into Brauer's staircase; or, as some say, straight through the adjacent door which leads to the Master's Lodge. Entirely unworthy of a scientific conference, I fear."

"Alas! Poor Ghost!"

"Precisely. Now this is your way—through the arch. Here's First Court, and there are your rooms, embowered in pink roses and moonlight. That light there is in the conference office showing that the worthy Willow is still labouring for our pleasure. Good night. Sweet dreams."

So Colonel Vorloff climbed the stairs of C staircase, and Davie returned to his rooms in Baxter's Court, and, when he had made himself a cup of tea, retired to bed to read the last fifty pages of *This Way to the Gallows*. He normally read three detective novels a week, and was a great one for spotting the villain several chapters before the author intended.

"This way to the Amaranthine fields," said Davie twenty minutes later as he snipped off the light. For him that was never a protracted journey—just long enough, this midnight, to examine his own small problem. Zinty and Krasner: old prison camp companions. They had a plan. It wasn't easy. Krasner was a caricaturist and had travelled in South America. Zinty was a doctor. Unless he'd forgotten something it didn't seem, so far, to be very mysterious after all.

VIII

At about the time that Dr. Davie reached the borders of sleep, Mostyn-Humphries (who had been compelled to evade Mr. Jump by climbing into college) was just turning out of the cloisters into his staircase, when he barged into one of the symposium visitors, descending the stairs as delicately as Agag. Both men gasped simultaneously. Then "Poof!" said the stranger. "You gave me a fright!"

"Sorry, sir," said Mostyn-Humphries. "You scared me too. I thought you were the college ghost. Lucky I know who you really are."

"Let me see," said the apparition. "At first it is a little confusing. First Court is to the left, and Baxter's Court straight on?"

"That's it," said Mostyn-Humphries. "Good night."

Saturday

I

For many years it had been Davie's habit to walk round the Fellows' Garden after breakfast. Today he meant to stay there until the delegates had all gone to ground, well out of the way in the New Court lecture room. The fact was he meant to play truant. Dr. Thomas J. Burgenheimer of some distant American university called to him in vain. He was not going.

Davie opened the garden door cautiously, skirted First Court, and entered Baxter's Court. But he had not stayed in the garden quite long enough. Through the neighbouring arch—the one connecting Baxter's Court with Cloister Court by way of the undercroft—came Dr. Zinty, walking extremely fast in the direction of his rooms.

"Hallo, sir!" said Davie brazenly. "Not evading the first lecture, I trust."

Zinty stopped, turned, and blushed like a child.

"No, indeed. I was looking for Dr. Brauer. He's not in his rooms."

"He'll be over at the lecture room in New Court. The session begins at nine-thirty today."

"Oh—so that's it: I wondered where everyone was. I thought it was at a quarter to ten."

"No—nine-thirty. Don't miss a moment. Dr. Burgenheimer is the supreme authority on—on whatever it is he's talking about. Enjoy yourself. Unfortunately I have an engagement."

And then Davie went back to his rooms, chose himself a gray hat with a wide brim, settled an orange-pink rosebud in his buttonhole, and set off aimlessly into a Cambridge miraculously empty. The undergraduates were nearly all down, and the charabancs with their burden of tourists had not yet turned up. Cambridge was quiet, fresh, and beautiful, and for half an hour he pottered happily among books and flowers in the marketplace.

Then it occurred to him to visit the Missionary Exhibition, which was in a small room in a side street behind the Guildhall. Davie was not particularly interested in missionaries and he disliked exhibitions, but he had promised Miss Ramble he would go, and go he must.

Miss Ramble was delighted. "Dr. Davie, how good of you to come!"

"Alas, Miss Ramble, few men have more leisure than myself. It is good of you to provide something new for my failing intellect to enjoy. Now what have you got to show me?"

"Start here, Dr. Davie, work your way round the room, and visit the central case last. That's how the catalogue goes. From costume—rather sparse I am afraid, just a few beads—through cooking utensils to music, and so on to weapons—all those dreadful clubs and spears and blowpipes. I'm afraid that's what interests people most. Violence has a sort of appeal. Poor Mrs. Courtney could hardly drag the children away. Then, in the center, photographs of the work, a model of a typical Borneo mission station, carvings made by the children, examples of weaving and pottery."

"Thank you, Miss Ramble, it all sounds very interesting."

"It is. It is. Everybody says so. Mr. Cowl was most impressed."

"He's been, has he?"

"Yes, and he says he may come again."

"Good Gracious! It just shows that there are no limits to the mysteries of Man. I would have thought Mr. Cowl and missionary exhibitions were poles apart."

Davie moved slowly round the room, dutifully looking at everything, but, as Miss Ramble had remarked, it was the weapons which were the most interesting.

"I never can imagine how those things work," he said.

"What? Blow-pipes?"

"Yes. I would have thought that the amount of puff that an ordinary person could impart would be just enough to dislodge the dart, and that it would fall out at one's feet. But no—it goes whizzing off like a bullet."

"I expect they're trained to it and have extra-special lungs."

"A Wagnerian soprano might shoot one of those things through an oak door, I don't doubt—but they can't be all like that."

"I believe it's easier than you think. It's something to do with compressed air. After all, Dr. Davie—pea-shooters—"

"Ah! There you have me. I recollect pea-shooters clearly. They certainly worked."

II

Miss Ramble had asked Geoffrey Willow to include one of her leaflets in the envelope supplied to each delegate, along with the program and the brief guide to Cambridge and the pin-on name and the invitation to the Master's garden party. And after the afternoon meeting several members of the conference had thought it worthwhile to visit the exhibition.

Miss Banbury and Miss Eggar were like oil and vinegar, but they had arrived together, had stayed together, and like oil and vinegar they went well together. So, after disagreeing on the merits of the Bridge of Sighs and Trinity Great Court and Clare and King's Chapel, they visited Miss Ramble's exhibition and enjoyed disagreeing about that too.

Miss Banbury thought that much work for good was being done for a primitive people. Miss Eggar wanted to know why we couldn't leave primitive peoples alone. "The only thing that Europe has done for the Far East is to make them a present of influenza and venereal disease," said Miss Eggar.

"But the mission hospital—" began Miss Ramble.

"Wouldn't have been necessary a hundred years ago, I'll bet."

"You must allow that the schools—"

"Nonsense! They're all acquiring a lot of useless knowledge such as how to use a sewing machine, and who won the battle of Trafalgar, and how many pennies go to a shilling, and forgetting how to catch octopuses and how to make their own remarkably hideous pottery."

"Now there you *are* wrong," said Miss Ramble. "Case 5 has some very fine examples of decorated dishes, and the last case but one, before you come to the blow-pipes, actually has a knife which the native boys use against the octopuses."

"My details are often wrong," said Miss Eggar, unabashed—

"Nearly always," said Miss Banbury.

"But my theories are sound. I accept your octopus knife *and* maintain that we should leave these excellent people alone."

" 'Happy the people whose annals are blank in history books,' " said Miss Ramble brightly.

"Nonsense," said Miss Eggar. "Carlyle was an old fool. So was Dryden with his 'When wild in woods the noble savage ran.' Everyone knows the poor wretch was running away from other noble savages—"

"And bears," said Miss Banbury.

"They were making history all right but there didn't happen to be anyone around to read it. They weren't any happier than we are."

"Aren't you contradicting yourself a little?" asked Miss Banbury.

"Very probably. I really can't remember how this conversation began."

"Octopus knives, I think," said Miss Ramble with a nervous laugh.

"I want to see the blow-pipes," said Miss Eggar.

"Everyone does!" cried Miss Ramble, flapping her hands in imitation despair, and leading the way across the room to the largest glass case. "Everyone wants to see the blow-pipes. The native arts go for nothing. A Hungarian visitor was here this afternoon—"

"Colonel Vorloff, I expect," said Miss Banbury.

"He was most interested because his work had taken him to this territory."

"Colonel Vorloff certainly," said Miss Eggar.

"He said he had actually used one of these dreadful things."

"Not more dreadful than an ordinary gun, when you come to think of it," said Miss Eggar. "It's curious how sinister any weapon becomes when it's wielded by a naked man with a bone through his nose in a jungle. For my part I'd as soon be killed by a poisoned arrow as by a sawn-off shotgun. At least a poisoned arrow does the job quickly."

When Colonel Vorloff had called at the exhibition he had been on his way to keep his engagement with Brauer at the laboratory and he was on his way back to St. Nicholas's when he overtook the two ladies.

"We've both been at that exhibition," began Miss Banbury.

"And we gathered that we had just missed you."

"The lady in charge said you knew how to use a blow-pipe. Do you really?"

"It's not difficult."

"Did you learn to do it just to see if you could?" asked Miss Eggar. "Or did you actually go out hunting and shooting things?"

"I have shot a tiger which would certainly have killed me if I hadn't got him first."

"Not with a blow-pipe?"

"No—a rifle."

"Then you haven't answered my question."

"I was on the way to do so. I have shot things with a rifle in self-defense. But I can't go out hunting things in cold blood. I'm too fond of animals. I only aimed a blow-pipe at tree trunks."

"Did you hit them?" persisted Miss Eggar.

"Yes. I'm a good shot. But the only animal I've wanted to kill is Man—Man, when I see him ill-treating some other animal."

"There's not much of that in this country," said Miss Banbury.

"I would say there was more than you think. Beating animals and starving them isn't the only way of ill-treating them. And some ways are legal."

"You mean laboratory cats and dogs?" said Miss Banbury. "I've never been happy about them."

"It's no good being sentimental about animals," said Miss Eggar. "Man comes first."

They had reached the entrance to the college, and, as there was still an hour to dinner-time, Miss Banbury and Miss Eggar went on down the lane to their lodgings. Colonel Vorloff turned down the long flagged walk which led to the great gate.

Inside his private cavern Mr. Jump was passing the time of day with one of the bed-makers.

"Well," said Mrs. Tibbs, as Vorloff passed the lodge window, "that's a cross-looking devil."

"What can you expect?" said Mr. Jump loftily. "In a few days he'll going back to Europe or some place. These people don't know what it's like to be free, and when they come to England they either don't approve or they're so surprised they don't want to go home again."

"You never said a truer word, Mr. Jump," said Mrs. Tibbs. "Give me our own people every time."

Halfway across First Court Vorloff met Dr. Davie.

"And how was the laboratory?" asked Davie.

Vorloff did not reply at once. First he looked back towards the great gate; then at the cobbles that flanked the stone path; then he looked Davie in the eyes.

"I know these places are legal and properly supervised," he said. "I know opinion is against me. But for my part I don't want to be helped that way."

"I understand your feelings exactly."

"Men like Dr. Brauer have saved the human race centuries of misery. I well believe it. But it makes me feel ashamed."

"I'm sorry you went."

"I'm not. If one doesn't face these things one doesn't know."

Davie cast around for a change of subject.

"Come into the Fellows' Garden," he said. "I'll show you the crankiest mulberry tree you ever saw. Every year the kitchens make mulberry jam and we all get a jar. That's the sort of thing that's so agreeable about a college existence. Special privileges. Of course when the reformers get to know of it mulberry jam will be doomed."

Sunday

I

Mrs. Courtney's garden party was on Sunday afternoon. The great plane tree on the lawn could have sheltered a hundred, and there the majority of the guests were assembled. It was hot outside those green curtains. Besides, that was where the food was. And food was the subject of the conversation. Abundance had suggested to someone a distant memory of wartime restrictions. What had the butter ration been? Something fantastic like two ounces a week. And then Mrs. Courtney started talking about the war before that.

"When rations were getting short in the old war," she said, "someone in Holland thought it would be a good plan to have a nice dish of bulbs. It wasn't, of course. I remember reading about it as a child. And there was an old gentleman in England who felt his rhubarb plant might be put to fuller uses. So he had the leaves served up like spinach."

"Oxalic acid," said Cowl.

"So sad, don't you think?" said Mrs. Courtney, helping herself to a lettuce sandwich. "It always seems to me miraculous that the human race survived at all. We know about yew and deadly nightshade—but there are all sorts of harmless-looking things which are absolutely lethal, and it must have been by trying them that people found out. Mr. Cowl . . . you know much more about botany than mathematics— ("Thank you," said Cowl gravely) —do tell us what *are* the things we mustn't eat."

"Practically everything," said Cowl. "Even the lettuce (which I see you are enjoying at this moment) contains oxalic acid."

"So does spinach," said Miss Eggar.

"Just think of those poor people who lived in those awful stone huts on top of Dartmoor—"

"My wife is referring to Neolithic Man," said Dr. Courtney.

"What a relief it must have been to discover that those delicious whortleberries were suitable for the children."

"And what a disappointment," said Miss Eggar, "when they discovered that ivy berries were not."

"One of our modern poets," said Cowl, "has written of *Salads of lilies and ballads of wine.*"

"Now this I like," said Miss Marden.

"As a line," said Cowl, "perhaps you do. As a salad you wouldn't."

"Especially lilies of the valley," said Miss Eggar grimly, "with perhaps a garnish of chopped foxglove leaves, and a few nice laburnum seeds."

"It will save the undertakers a lot of trouble, Mrs. Courtney, if you stay in your vegetable garden," said Cowl. "Even then," persisted Miss Eggar in a sepulchral voice, "avoiding sprouting potato tubers."

"People have eaten aconite before now in mistake for horseradish," said Cowl.

"Aconite?" said Mrs. Courtney anxiously.

"Commonly called Wolfsbane or Monkshood: the name's a warning in itself."

"*Salads of lilies,*" murmured Dr. Davie, "what a title for a detective story!"

"I was at that Missionary Exhibition yesterday," said Miss Banbury. "It's strange, isn't it, that primitive people, all over the world, have discovered the same sort of deadly arrow poison. It can't always be from the same sort of plant."

"In Kenya," said Miss Eggar, "it's a tree known to Europeans as the candelabra tree, because its branches stick up like one of those things one sees standing in a cathedral chancel. They pep it up with some muck they get from stewed beetles."

"Those little men in the Kalahari desert," said Colonel Vorloff, "make poison by distilling the grubs they find behind the bark of a tree; insects often come into it but the worst poisons generally come from a root, or the bark of a root."

"It's a root," said Willow, "that's the principal ingredient of the Somaliland stuff. As a matter of fact I've seen it made."

"I bet you have," said Miss Marden, and "Now we're off," said Miss Eggar turning to Jones-Herbert, who happened to be standing next to her. Jones-Herbert went bright pink. He did not want to be associated with sallies of that kind.

"There's a tree called wabai, and the Midgan people make a poison from it called wabaio. They dig up a root and chop off its bark and cook it up with some other wood called dukneya, I think."

"Dukneya is right," said Signor Bondini unexpectedly.

"Goodness!" said the Master. "Another poisoner in our midst."

"Somaliland and Italy," said Bondini, waving his hands in an effort to amplify his words. "I was official, you know."

"Ah, yes," said the Master. "Well, Willow, what do you do with the wabai and the dukneya?"

"You simmer it over some other wood—very special, but I think that part of the recipe's probably superstitious. It thickens down to a sort of brown gravy and smells horrible. When it's fresh it's lethal and acts instantaneously. A bird or a small animal dies in a matter of seconds. It takes longer on a big animal or a man—but not much."

Krasner leaned forward from behind Yana Marden. "I'm not a toxicologist," he said, "so I can't discuss the finer points of the receipt—but it must have been made in much the same way in the Amazon forest. I have often seen the Jivaro Indians making the blow-gun, and using it. Their poison also comes from the bark of two trees. The recipe is a secret and the monopoly of certain families. The Jivaro don't make it. They have to get it by barter. But they also have a secret of their own. They make the stuff even stronger by brewing large ants and adding the juice to the curare."

"Fiends!" murmured Mrs. Courtney.

"Aren't those the people who shrink heads?" asked Miss Banbury.

"One of them," said Krasner. "And I've seen them do that, too."

"Really!" Mrs. Courtney broke out. "This is the most horrible conversation."

"You started it," said the Master.

"I didn't think a harmless remark about rhubarb leaves would reveal the entire party as a coven of warlocks and witches. If Richard had been here our lives wouldn't have been worth a fig. Catherine dear, do say something quite different."

"As a matter of fact," said Catherine, "I did want to ask about Dr. Brauer's lecture on Monday. Do you think, Master, we might be allowed to decorate the dais a bit—you know, screens on either side to cover the Combination Room door, and the scaffolding on the window—and, if possible have some plants, or something."

"You must ask the college president," said the Master, waving a hand in the direction of Davie.

"I don't remember it being done before," said Davie, "but I don't see any objection."

"Thank you very much," said Catherine.

"I might see if I could procure some deadly night-shade," said Cowl. "And stinking hellebore—now that's a charming plant and most suitable to the occasion."

Mrs. Courtney shook her finger at him. "It's a very good idea, Catherine. The dais is too wide. I'm sure Westlake can be persuaded to bring us all sorts of things from the greenhouse."

"Provided that Richard hasn't blown them all up," said Davie who was looking across the garden to where the children were digging a hole in one of the more distant flower beds.

"There's Dr. Brauer," said Mrs. Courtney. "He's usually late. I don't think he likes social engagements, poor man, and cuts them as short as he can."

Several ladies slightly adjusted their positions on the lawn, so that Brauer unconsciously walked into the usual circle of admirers. But Dr. Brauer was plainly tired and not in much mood for gallantry.

"Tea," said Mrs. Courtney.

"That's the one thing I do want," said Brauer, as though rejecting the entire company.

"I shall have to get into the magic enclosure somehow," said Junge to Davie. "Dr. Brauer is so busy and so elusive I can never get hold of him."

"Wasn't he in on Friday evening?" asked Davie.

"No."

"Well, catch him now. I expect he'll be grateful to you. He doesn't really want to be a pin-up."

"Pin-up" was not in Dr. Junge's vocabulary. Davie apologized and explained. Dr. Junge glanced swiftly round the assembled faces. "I would say these pin-ups are rather rare among us, wouldn't you?" he whispered.

"Except perhaps—"

"Miss Marden?" said Junge. "Yes. I agree there."

"Come along," said Davie. "Let us be bold. Brauer —here's somebody you haven't met: Dr. Junge from Munich."

Krasner and Zinty had been walking round the garden by opposite paths. They met where the lawn ran alongside the east end of the fourteenth-century chapel. It was a remote corner of the garden out of the sunshine.

"When was it you called on him?" asked Krasner.

"Yesterday—early."

"Time enough surely for some result."

"Well it depends whether—"

"That's what's wrong with your plan, as I always said. 'It depends.' It may work. It may not. The other idea is better. It's direct."

"And dangerous."

"Not necessarily."

"I don't think we better stand here talking," said Zinty.

So Krasner went on round the garden till he happened to meet Miss Marden, and Zinty went on in the other direction till he happened to meet Miss Eggar.

"Whither away?" said Miss Eggar.

"Looking for Mrs. Courtney. It's time to go."

"I was looking," said Miss Eggar, "for something lethal to put in Dr. Brauer's tea. He's too arrogant, don't you think? But perhaps you don't. There's Mrs. Courtney over there if you really want her."

Mrs. Courtney had thought it would be pleasant to invite a few of the undergraduates, but they had not made much effort to mix with the visitors, and after assuaging the pangs of hunger had mostly wandered off along the gravelled paths.

"And what are you doing?" said Mostyn-Humphries to Richard Courtney.

"I'm getting a land mine right under that rose bush," said Richard.

"And then Richard's going to blackmail old West-lake," said Abel.

"Be quiet, Abel," said Clarissa.

"He is. And when old Westlake says we're not to do something, then Richard's going to say 'All right, then we'll blow up the rose bush' and that's how we'll get what we want."

"And very good reasoning, too," said Mostyn-Humphries, adding, as he and Baggs strolled down the path, "You see, my venerable Baggs, it's in the blood. If you don't get what you want you blow the other chap up. You peace-at-all-price chaps haven't a ruddy earthly. You're always in retreat. You mean well, but you're only helping the other side."

"I don't agree. We've got to stop that bomb."

"Which reminds me—how are your plans advancing in that respect?"

"You'll see. It won't be much—but you shan't say I didn't have a bang at it."

"Bang! I adore that unerring instinct of yours for the most unsuitable word."

"Oh stow it!" said Baggs. "Here comes Brauer."

Brauer was advancing slowly down the path in the company of Dr. Junge.

Mostyn-Humphries had nothing against Brauer except that, keeping in the set below his, he had been passing him in the cloisters for two years and had grown tired of the possible permutations upon "Good morning" and "Good evening." Brauer was not a man to get friendly with undergraduates.

So, "Come on," said Mostyn-Humphries, "how right you are. I particularly want to draw your attention to the *digitalis purpurea* prominently displayed in yonder bed. *Digitalis* (as no doubt you are aware) is a sub-order of the *scrophularineae*—plants purgative, emetic, bitter and poisonous. The leaves, as you were so rightly about to observe, my dear Baggs, are rugose and radical petrioled, while the upper cauline is sessile. The flowers are pendulous, and the calex-lobes oblong-lanceolate. The whole thing, as Sir James Hooker so finely puts it, is stout and erect. Etymology not what you so regrettably expected, but *digitus* meaning a finger, and even that refers to the flower—hence 'gloves.' "

"Oh, stow it!" said Baggs. "I want to go. Do we have to say goodbye properly on this sort of lark?"

"It's preferred so," said Mostyn-Humphries.

Brauer and Junge had been talking together for fifteen minutes when Caldecott joined them beside a big dahlia bed.

"I don't like those tall ones with open petals," said Junge. "Those small round ones are the pretty ones. I like the way they're all folded up."

"I believe 'convolute' is the word," said Caldecott. "And a very nice botanical adjective it is too."

"I must be getting back," Brauer said. "I've got work to do."

"Work?" said Caldecott. "This is very serious. Do you mean to tell me that your lecture isn't ready yet?"

"I'm not going to tell you anything, Caldecott. Goodbye, Junge."

"I'll hope to see you tomorrow then," said Junge. "Or Tuesday."

The party was certainly over. Some of the guests had already left, the others were heading for the ornamental gate that separated the Master's garden from the entrance to the college.

As Davie was walking under the tower gateway Brauer caught up with him.

"Davie—"

"Brauer—"

"I—I wondered—could you spare me some time this evening. I want to have a private talk with you. I need your advice."

"I don't know that I'm particularly wise, Brauer. Only old. But if I can help you I'll do my best."

"I know you can."

"But—oh dear!—not tonight, dear man. I'm sorry, but I'm dining in Corpus. You could come now of course, but I haven't long, and I must change."

"I don't want to talk in a hurry."

"What about tomorrow evening after Hall? You can have all the time you want then."

Brauer hesitated. "I don't have to go to the morning lecture. Could I come then? I don't want to go all through the day turning these matters over in my head. I'm terribly tired and it's more important than I can explain."

"Do come then, Brauer. What time? Ten o'clock?"

"I'd rather not meet people."

"All right—ten-fifteen. They'll all be in the lecture room by then. And look here—I'll come to you."

"That would be kind. Thank you. Thank you very much."

"Sorry you're so bothered, Brauer. But—as those awful little funny cards say, 'It may never happen.'"

"That's just it," said Brauer. "I'm afraid it will."

II

Shortly after two o'clock in the morning, Mostyn-Humphries, who had been spending a pleasant evening on the river with Tilly Pool, the prettiest of the waitresses at The Cosy Pantry, made his way over the spikes that separate the Close from New Court. He had run out of conversation with Tilly two hours before, but climbing into college had great charms for Mostyn-Humphries. It prepared him for a good night's sleep. Solemn scholars might sleep the sleep of the justified after a long evening's swot. Mostyn-Humphries liked to sleep the sleep of the undetected. He let himself down cautiously among the evergreen shrubs, and passed quietly under a small archway that opened on Baxter's Court. And there he stopped. Behind the scaffolding the oriel window glittered in the moonlight; and from the foot of the ladder a figure scuttled into the shadows that led to the cloisters.

Mostyn-Humphries glanced up at the scaffold poles. "My poor sweet Baggs," he whispered, "the prize for the lad least likely to succeed is yours for the taking."

Monday

I

For the few who happened to see it the beginning of a remarkable day was the discovery at breakfast time of a small streamer sagging between two poles of the scaffold outside the oriel window. It was Baggs' contribution to world peace, and it said "Ban the Bomb."

The second porter, unnecessarily directed from the ground by Mr. Jump, had it down in no time.

The only other people to receive the message were Miss Banbury and Miss Eggar, who had reached the college a little early and were taking a stroll before breakfast.

"It doesn't say whose bomb," said Miss Banbury.

"Really!" said Miss Eggar. "Are you being irritating on purpose?"

"No," said Miss Banbury. "It is a natural affliction. But it does seem to me to be important."

And not many people saw the small but more interesting announcement in the local papers concerning a burglary at the Missionary Exhibition.

"'Except for a brief absence for a cup of tea,' Miss Ramble informed our special reporter, 'I was present throughout the day. No suspicious characters visited the exhibition, indeed the majority of our visitors were persons known to me. Yet at the close of the day I found one of the glass cases had been broken and one of the small native weapons had been abstracted.'"

"Abstracted," murmured Davie. "Admirable word."

Cowl entered the Combination Room.

"I suppose it is you, Cowl, who's been breaking into Miss Ramble's exhibition and abstracting her native weapon."

"Her *what?*"

Davie explained.

"Miss Ramble said you'd been at the exhibition," he added, looking severely over the top of his glasses. "And what's more she said you meant to go again."

"Good heavens! How that female twists one's words. She bullied me into going, and then, when I left, she said, 'Do come again. One can't take it all in at once.'"

"And you said?"

"Something feeble like 'I will if I can.'"

"H'm," said Davie. "I'm afraid that isn't going to do you any good at the trial." Cowl hit him over the head with *The Times*.

"And what are you doing here anyhow?" said Davie. "I consider it a very suspicious circumstance. You ought to be at the conference."

"And you?"

"Oh—I'm entirely supernumerary. I go when I feel like it."

"And you don't?"

"I don't. I have an engagement. And it's time I went. Good morning, Cowl, and do try to keep out of further mischief."

II

The last bed-makers left their keys with Mr. Jump at the porter's lodge, and drifted up the Long Walk to St. Nicholas Lane, and suddenly the college lay silent and peaceful in the sunshine. Nobody was about except Westlake and his attendant boy who were quietly planting out chrysanthemums. From the Close came the pleasant whirring of a lawnmower and at about eleven o'clock the distant plonk of a tennis ball indicated that Baggs had successfully been seduced from his work by Mostyn-Humphries.

At eleven-thirty Mr. Jump walked purposefully across First Court in the direction of the Buttery. At eleven-forty-five he walked back again. At twelve o'clock Cowl returned to his staircase. He had listened to the eleven o'clock paper, but was cutting the discussion. At the top of the first flight he paused for a minute outside Brauer's door. Brauer was talking to Davie. Cowl did not listen at doors and peep through keyholes as a rule. But the words were not without interest to him.

"You think you are actually in danger?"

Then, feeling a bit of a slut, he plodded up the next flight to his own set.

At twelve-thirty Catherine came down the Long Walk. She was having lunch with Mrs. Courtney. Mr. Jump, who was standing at the doorway of his cavern, looked at her with disapproval. Slacks. If one of his bed-maker acquaintances had been present he would certainly have invited her to tell him what next. But as there was no one at hand to support him with "Ah, you're right there, Mr. Jump," he contented himself with lifting his top hat with a Judas-like smile.

"Good morning, Mr. Jump," said Catherine, opening the gate to the Lodge garden.

"Good morning, madam," replied Mr. Jump, adding under his breath, "Ussey!"

And then at twelve-thirty-five Cloister Court and Baxter's Court were suddenly full of delegates on their way to Hall. But, since at that moment no one had thoughts for anything but lunch, First Court

still lay empty, except when Colonel Vorloff returned
to his rooms to leave a notebook and pick up a
handkerchief and Dr. Junge went back to change
into a cooler jacket. It was, he thought, as he peered
out of his rose-framed window, a most delightful
and civilized scene. Below him the turf lay exquis-
itely striped by the mower in two shades of green.
Beyond the flower beds on the right the Close reced-
ed in a mystery of trees. Across the angle of the
court he could see Davie standing at Brauer's window
—but Davie must have descended G staircase at the
same time as Junge and Vorloff returned from their
rooms, for all three met a minute later at the end
of the queue on the Hall staircase.

"And now," said Davie, "for a nice salad of lilies.
If you'll sit by me we might even have a ballad of
wine together."

III

As soon as lunch had been cleared Catherine and
Mrs. Courtney began to arrange the dais for the lecture. Screens were brought in from the Lodge, and
set on either side like wings on a stage, and an unwilling college gardener had arrived with a load of
ferns and pot-plants.

"It really is very good of Westlake," said Mrs. Courtney. "I shall beg Richard to take his land mine out
of that rose bed. We must express our gratitude
somehow."

"Can I help?"

Dr. Junge was smiling in the doorway.

"Thank you," said Catherine, and "Why aren't
you being lectured at?" asked Mrs. Courtney.

"There's nothing till Dr. Brauer's lecture," said

Catherine. "One must ease off at the end of a conference or they all want to commit murder."

"Your husband has a kind heart, Mrs. Willow,"
said Junge.

"He's been to a few and he knows." Catherine was
walking slowly down the left-hand wall, scrutinizing
the screens. Near the front she stopped. "I can still
see through, Adela. It doesn't cover off. The back
one needs to come out a bit."

"Let me help," said Junge.

"Thank you so much. They are a bit heavy," said
Mrs. Courtney.

"That right?"

"A little more. Stop! That's it."

"What about the window side?"

"Yes," said Mrs. Courtney. "We must cover that
awful scaffolding."

"I was only thinking of the door," said Catherine.
"Sorry. Will you help again?"

"That it?" said Junge. "Yes?"

"Out a bit—no, that's too far. Right."

"Why, that's beautiful."

Mrs. Courtney turned round.

Miss Marden was standing in the doorway with
Krasner. "We meant to help and we're too late. That's
my large sin. I'm always late. I shall probably be
too late for the Day of Judgment."

"Never mind," said Mrs. Courtney, adjusting a
dahlia to the new position of the screen. "You meant
to help and that is what matters. I do think it looks
rather nice, don't you? I only hope those terrible
children won't get in and do anything funny."

"Such as?" said Miss Marden.

"Oh—you know—such as cushions that squeak when
you get up, and bottles of water that won't pour
out. That sort of thing. They will do it. When old

Dr. Finn dined at the Lodge last year they managed to give him a sham glass of champagne and the poor old dear was quite a quarter of an hour trying to get something out of it before Clive noticed. So unkind, don't you think?"

"Which reminds me," said Catherine. "There ought to be a glass and a bottle of water on the table. Don't bother. I'll get it."

So Mrs. Courtney went back to the Lodge, and Krasner, Miss Marden, and Dr. Junge made their way to the Close. And Catherine went for the water.

When she re-entered the Hall three minutes later Colonel Vorloff was standing by the screen on the oriel window side of the dais, looking at the pictures behind the high table.

"Hullo, Colonel Vorloff," said Catherine. "What are you up to?"

"I've been meaning to have a proper look at the pictures and the window ever since we arrived," he answered. "And now it's nearly time that we went. Don't you think there's something very gemütlich about Bishop Allbottel? It's a face I find consoling in an unsympathetic world."

"Yes," said Catherine. "He's got the beginning of a smile which seems to say 'I know—but don't worry. I won't tell.'"

"In that case a friend to everybody," said Vorloff.

"Are you coming for a stroll in the Close?" said Catherine. "That's where most of the others are."

"That will be very pleasant, Mrs. Willow."

So the two of them left the Hall. And Westlake came in and removed the empty boxes which had contained the pot-plants.

Presently the Combination Room door opened, and Geoffrey Willow made his way on to the dais. He looked approvingly at the flowers and the screens, slightly adjusted the lectern and the chair beside it, walked halfway down the Hall, viewed the dais from the right side and then from the left, walked to the door and surveyed the scene again. That was just like him. Everyone agreed that Geoffrey Willow was a first-rate organizer. He never left anything to chance.

IV

After lunch Dr. Davie had gone back to his rooms and indulged in a nap with such nice timing that when he awoke it was twenty-five minutes after three. By the time he reached the Hall it was nearly full, but in the empty space at the back several delegates were still standing. Vorloff, who was talking to Junge and Dr. Burgenheimer, waved a hand towards a chair, and Willow came down the gangway to tell Davie there was a seat in the third row. But at this late hour Davie was unwilling to press forward, and he had remembered the little stone gallery at the back of the Hall. Rather like and no bigger than a theater box, it protruded slightly into the Hall, and five hundred years earlier had been the Prior's means of observing his monks at table. It was not open to the public, but as a member of the college Davie could go there, and half a minute later he had himself nicely placed, sole observer of everybody in the Hall—except of those who might still be standing at the back.

As the chapel clock struck three-thirty Dr. Courtney and Brauer walked on to the dais from the Combination Room. While the Master spoke neatly of Brauer's accomplishments Brauer produced his little bottle, took out a tablet, and dropped it in his glass of water. But the Master was a mercifully brief chair-

man, and before Brauer had time to drink Dr. Courtney was informing the audience that he would not
stand between them and their pleasure any longer.
Then he took his seat in the front row and Brauer
rose on the flowery dais and began to speak.

It was a compelling and beautiful voice, but Davie
was not a scientist and it was not long before his
attention wandered to the flowers and the screens. As
his eyes moved to the right they were suddenly engaged by what seemed to be a slow movement just
behind the top of the back screen. Someone had come
late, presumably, and was insanely trying to enter
the Hall by the Combination Room door. Down on
the floor the door was not visible but up here in the
gallery one got a clear view of the top few inches.
Davie could see the door open, but he could not see
who it was who had opened it and must now be
standing concealed from the audience but in full view
of the speaker. And so it was that of all the people
in the Hall only Davie understood why Brauer's attention was suddenly distracted and his head turned
sharply to his left. A look of annoyance passed over
his face, but having been halted he made the inter-
ruption more natural by taking a drink from the
glass at his side. Then he set the glass down, lifted
his hand suddenly to the back of his head as though
he were warding off a mosquito, brought his hand
down, cleared his throat and began again. But at the
end of three sentences the strong voice faltered. For
a moment he swayed and then suddenly collapsed.
As he fell he knocked against the table. The glass
shattered on the floor. The bottle of tablets rolled
between the screens.

The quiet room suddenly seemed to explode. People started out of their seats. Exclamations, reserved
and small in themselves, amalgamated like a whistle

of steam. As there was nothing he could do Davie stood watching the extraordinary picture, saw a white-faced Zinty leap eagerly to his feet and clap a hand to his mouth as though to prevent himself screaming; saw the Master and Cowl and Caldecott and one or two others step quickly on to the dais; saw Parkin of Caius kneel down beside Brauer; saw that somehow or other Miss Banbury had got to the far side of Brauer and was supporting his head on her right arm; and that Miss Eggar, who was standing in the background, was leaning down and picking up bits of broken glass which she put out of harm's way on the table. Brauer must have cut himself already in falling for there was blood on the handkerchief which Miss Banbury was pressing against his neck. Then Willow, who must have been standing out of Davie's sight under the gallery, pushed forward and joined the group on the dais.

For a moment or two the Hall became tensely quiet. Then the Master approached the front of the dais.

"Ladies and Gentlemen," he said, "I am sorry to tell you that we are in the presence of a grave tragedy. Dr. Brauer is dead. Those who knew him were well aware that his heart had been giving him much cause for alarm. I shall be grateful if you will leave the Hall. The meeting, and indeed our conference, is closed."

"So's the door," said Davie to himself. "The Combination Room door. It's closed again."

"Some of you," the Master went on, "will probably wish to leave the college now. But should that be inconvenient I hope you will believe that you are very welcome to retain your rooms till tomorrow."

Davie left the little gallery and hastened downstairs. As he passed the Hall he noticed Bondini standing on the threshold of the open door, behind him a mass of moving heads and shoulders. He hurried on down the main staircase and at the bottom ran into Catherine and Junge.

"Dr. Junge says Dr. Brauer's been taken ill," she said.

"Worse than that, Catherine. He's dead."

"Oh—goodness! I was going to look for Geoffrey."

"Yes, do do that."

Catherine turned and ran up the stairs, followed by Junge. And Davie, twisting into the cloisters, walked along one side to the door leading to the Combination Room. Through the arcade on the far side he caught a glimpse of Richard (who had no right to be there), waving a club like a savage. But fortunately Richard did not see Dr. Davie, and so, unimpeded, Dr. Davie was back at the other end of the Hall two minutes after leaving the Gallery.

The Master was giving instructions in a low voice to Mr. Jump, who had miraculously appeared from nowhere. Willow was kneeling beside Brauer, arranging a cloth which he had brought from the Combination Room. Catherine and Junge were standing just below the dais, looking at him. Miss Eggar was still studying the floor for pieces of broken glass. Miss Banbury, looking very pale, had retreated to the front row of seats and was sitting beside Mrs. Courtney. Colonel Vorloff, who must have followed Catherine up the Hall while Davie was crossing the cloisters was standing beside, almost behind, the screen by the oriel window. Parkin, Caldecott, Cowl. The rest of the audience was on their way out of the Hall, their backs to the dais. Except Zinty. He stood still, as though fascinated, biting one finger of his left hand, and with his right crushing a handkerchief into a ball. Then he turned very slowly and followed the rest of the company.

V

John Scobie, Brauer's doctor, was at home when the telephone rang, and he was round at the college almost as soon as the body had been carried to a temporary resting place in a ground-floor room. After his examination he called at the Lodge and found Davie sitting with the Master.

"He's been near to this several times," said Scobie. "Nothing unexpected about it. I can give a certificate."

"I'm glad of that," said the Master. "Post-mortems are unpleasant things. He seemed all right when he got up to speak. Then he took a drink from his glass of water—"

"Into which he'd put one of those tablets he always had," put in Davie.

"Did he? I didn't see that."

"And almost immediately after, he clutched his hand over his waistcoat, swayed and fell."

"Clot of blood," said Scobie. "Goes straight to the heart."

"To the ordinary uninstructed observer," Davie said, "there was something strangely coincidental in the drinking from the glass and the collapse. You don't think—"

"As the tablets are intended to relieve the patient, Dr. Davie, I don't see how there could be anything wrong there. But if you've still got the glass—"

"We haven't. It was knocked over and broken. But I picked up the bottle. Here you are. Would it perhaps be worthwhile testing them?"

The Master concealed a smile. He knew Davie's addiction to detective fiction.

Scobie looked at the bottle. "Seems all right," he said. "But you're quite right. I'll see about it."

After Scobie had gone Davie said, "There's something I ought to tell you, Master. It's an odd coincidence, but I happen to know that Brauer had an idea his life was in danger."

VI

Only a little over six hours before, Davie had called on Brauer as arranged, and "Well, what's this problem of yours, old friend?" he had asked.

Brauer's rooms were made beautiful by bright and delicate china, and a collection of glass which was famous enough to have been photographed and described more than once in the glossier collector's magazines. By arranging the pieces in attractive corner cupboards and cabinets Brauer had managed to conceal the extent of his riches. Nothing was on display. Everything was set out to please. Most of it was behind glass doors to preserve it from the attention of Mrs. Pilsworthy, the bed-maker; but there was one piece, not five inches high, which stood on the center of the chimney piece. Kneeling before one of those three-pronged, dead-white, Staffordshire tree stumps, two boys had paused on their way to school. One had a slate, the other three books strapped together—but these were laid aside and the boys were playing marbles. For that kind of porcelain it was remarkably natural, and yet made adorably conventional by the gold whorls and squiggles which the artist had contrived to include not only round the base but also on the tree. Brauer loved it better than any of his more valuable Chelsea figures, and he looked at it now as though it gave him confidence. Then he turned his tired eyes towards Davie.

"It's a long story, and it's been burning a hole in my heart for years. There was always the possibility that I would have to tell someone. Now I must . . ."

On the top of a neighbouring bookcase was a delicious Rockingham Cow with red-brown patches on her flanks and her feet bedded in a dark green pasture. Her horns were golden and her mouth was open, and Brauer, rejecting the milk jug, always liked to think she was mooing at the boys. He moved to the bookcase and minutely adjusted the cow's position. Then with his back to Davie, he said "Sometimes a man who has been in trouble changes his name. I changed mine."

"It must have been a long time ago," said Davie. "You've been here ten years and you were well-known in America before that."

Brauer returned to the high-backed chair at his table.

"Most men who change their names from a real name to an assumed one," he said. "I changed from an assumed name to my real one."

There did not seem any comment to make on that, and Davie made none.

"I am, as you know, a German. I was beginning to be known as a surgeon round about 1938. But I was against the Nazis and—not to bother you with the long horrid story of waiting for that midnight knock on the door—I landed up in a prison camp and finally in Auschwitz. You know about that ghastly place. All true. But there were good people there, not in authority but doing work under authority. I was due to be killed—but I had friends in the hospital block. It is an old trick—but it's worked on many occasions, owing to overcrowding and administrative muddle, and it worked for me. My friends substituted me for a Polish doctor who had died the day after reaching camp. I was kept in bed for some days, supposedly suffering from an infectious fever. The S.S. guards wouldn't come near the place. And in due course I emerged as another person. I was a Polish doctor, and I wore a small beard."

A square inside a circle inside a square inside a circle: Brauer leant forward, doodling on the blotting paper. Davie did not speak. Presently Brauer said, "I was a good surgeon."

"I'm sure you were."

Brauer paused for a full minute. Davie said nothing.

"I think you know what I'm going to say."

"Perhaps I do, Brauer."

"Under orders I had to perform operations on men and women. They were unjust, unfair, unforgivable."

"Don't tell me about it, Brauer, if it distresses you. I've read the books. I know as much as I want to know about the terrible Dr. Pavik and the rest of them. I suppose you knew him."

"Pavik?" Brauer shuddered. "It's terrible, absolutely terrible for me to have to talk about this."

"I'm sorry. I oughtn't to have brought Pavik into it."

"Pavik wasn't any worse than anyone else."

Brauer got up, walked across to the window—then walked slowly back to the fireplace. He looked at the boys playing marbles, and to Davie it seemed that the boys had stopped in their game to look at Brauer.

"The point is, Davie, I knew how to do it. If I'd refused I suppose I would have been killed. I don't know. Certainly, if I'd refused, the operations would have been worse done by someone else. I didn't bungle. And you must remember I wasn't a German any more; I was a despised Pole. At the end I got away before the Allied armies arrived. I shaved off my beard, and escaped as Dr. Brauer, the anti-Nazi who had been imprisoned by Hitler. It was true. Everyone knew it was true. Only three men at the hospital had known my secret. One died before the war ended. One was shot in the last days, trying to escape. The third man had not been a friend of mine. He'd become aware of the plot and had been persuaded to keep quiet. I worried about him for a long time; but the years passed and nothing happened. Gradually I forgot. I managed to get to America. At the War Crimes trials no one could find the Polish doctor. Naturally not. He was dead. Don't suppose I defend myself, Davie: but I have had to live with that for twenty years. I've paid all right. . . . Have a drink."

"Thank you," said Davie, not because he needed one but because he thought Brauer did.

When Brauer was back in his chair Davie said, You didn't ask me here to tell me only that."

"No."

Brauer paused: for a moment it seemed to Davie that he was uncertain how to go on, or if to go any further at all. He started doodling on the blotting paper again. A circle inside a square inside a circle inside a square. Then, "I had a shock on Friday evening at the cocktail party," he said. "I recognized somebody."

"Not this third man?"

"No—no—but it was a man from Auschwitz. I'm certain of it. I don't remember a thing about him except his face. I can see it now across twenty years. A terrible face. He was chattering something at me, protesting as far as he had strength. He tried to stop my work. I pushed him out of the room. People were always protesting. What was it possible to do? I can't even remember what it was about. And now he's here. I saw him looking at me. If he's not come here to identify me it's a pretty queer coincidence. It's terrible—after all these years to—"

"You mean—to get involved all over again in all the horrible aura of Dr. Pavik?"

"That, of course—but more too. When people are out for revenge they don't usually prefer legal processes."

"You think you are actually in danger?"

"I do."

"Which of the delegates is it?"

"I've been keeping out of the way and I don't want to ask questions. I'm not sure who he is."

"Where was he at the cocktail party?"

"When I saw him he was standing in the large window."

And then Davie remembered how Brauer had looked, as he thought, at Miss Marden. "It must have been Krasner, or Zinty, both from New York. Or Junge, who was behind them."

"Not Junge," said Brauer. "You introduced him to me at the garden party. I'd never met him before. It was one of those others."

Krasner and Zinty. From the first they had obtruded on Davie's attention. But Zinty had seemed a very pleasant creature at dinner that night. Was there a great deal behind those two—or was the unhappy Paul Brauer ill with imagined danger and ravaged conscience?

Brauer crossed to a Chippendale bureau and opened its slanting lid. "I want to show you where my will is, Davie." He pointed to a pigeonhole. "There. I've made you executor. I hope you don't mind. I ought to have asked you first, I know."

"That's all right, Brauer."

"My scientific papers are all at the laboratory. What's here is personal."

"And is that all you wanted to say?" Davie asked.

It must have been half a minute before Brauer answered him. Then he said, "There's a whole packet more, Davie, but there isn't time to talk about it now."

"Shall I come back?"

Brauer hesitated again. Davie could see that he didn't know which way to turn.

"After the lecture?"

"Thank you very much, Davie. Yes. I wish you would."

Davie got up and looked out of the window on to First Court. Colonel Vorloff and Dr. Junge were walking towards their rooms.

Looking the other way, Davie saw Mr. Jump bending a majestic ear to a little man in a silver-gray suit with a silver-gray tie. In his buttonhole he wore a large red rose and somehow Davie divined that behind the lapel the stalk of that rose was inserted into a little metal case containing a thimbleful of water. A perfectly sensible idea, and yet one from which Davie recoiled as readily as from that other eminently sensible device of the made-up bow tie. Mr. Jump waved a finger vaguely in Davie's direction. Davie promptly withdrew into the room.

"Hullo!" he said. "These are pretty. I haven't seen these before."

He was looking at half a dozen funnel-shaped wine glasses of that palest blue that proclaims Waterford. Each was engraved with the same device, a fox's head, but a different monogram. "Something new?"

"Er—yes," said Brauer, rather as though he didn't want to discuss the matter. "They're glasses that belonged to an eighteenth-century club—in Ireland—one for each member—supposed to be." And as that was all the information he seemed inclined to give, Davie continued—

"What are you doing for lunch?"

"I'm going to the Lodge."

"Of course. And you and the Master will come to the lecture together."

"Yes."

"Well—let's go down."

"I'm not quite ready," said Brauer. "There's still five minutes, and I must write a letter."

So Davie made his way down the steep little staircase, towards the bottom becoming aware of a pair of waiting legs.

"Sorry, sorry," said Davie. "No passing on these stairs, I'm afraid. Thank you."

"Excuse me," said the legs; "this is where Dr. Brauer lives, isn't it? Never seen such a rabbit warren. Do you know if he's in?"

It was the man in the silver-gray suit.

"Yes, yes. On the first floor. But you'll hardly catch him. He's just on his way to an engagement. That I know."

"Fair enough," said the man. "If I can see him for just a minute I dare say I can make an appointment for later."

"Ah yes—perhaps so."

"Thanks a lot," said the gray suit, and disappeared up the dark stair.

"God! What muck people talk!" muttered Davie as he walked along the cloister to join the queue on the Hall staircase. "What's fair? And enough for what?"

VII

"Brauer had an idea that his life was in danger," Davie said, and then regretted his words. The faint

possibility that Brauer's death had not been a natural one was no reason for betraying his confidence.
Not yet at any rate.

"Why on earth should he have thought that?"
asked the Master.

"Perhaps his nerves had twisted his imagination.
I don't know. But that's what he said—and only this
morning too."

"It looks as though anything Brauer had to fear
was forestalled by Death in one of his more usual
and accepted disguises."

"I hope so," said Davie. "Goodness! I hope so."

"I don't expect any complications—but if there are,
Davie, please keep a watching brief for me. I've got
to go up to London this evening. And it's time I was
going. I'll be back on the morning train. Goodbye
and thank you."

Davie left the Lodge by the cloister door and
turned immediately left into G staircase. He had the
keys of Brauer's rooms. The westering sun was staring in at the windows, and all the china figures stood
shining in the mellow light. Davie crossed to the
bureau and took out Brauer's will. It was in a long
envelope and sealed. It was difficult to believe that
he had been sitting in this quiet room so short a
time before, talking to the man who had once been
so ebullient, so handsome, so tall, and had looked
so deflated, so drawn, so bowed, as he sat at the
table doodling. A square inside a circle inside a
square inside a circle. Glancing down at the table
Davie noticed that at the center of one of these de-
vices Brauer had written in tiny characters the word
"Stumpf." At the center of another he had written
"Born." At the heart of three others was the name
"Pavik."

Poor Brauer! A many-sided man. What if he *had*
been "the Polish doctor"? That was a blot, but not

a blot that could totally obscure plain goodness of character.

VIII

Davie closed and locked Brauer's door, and came downstairs into the cloisters. Then he entered the stone tunnel by the buttery, passed the great Norman pillar by the Hall stairs, and emerged into the sunlight in Baxter's Court. The college seemed deserted. Presumably few of the delegates had availed themselves of the Master's invitation to stay. But as he entered his own staircase he noticed that the door of Zinty's room stood open, and he could see a suitcase on the floor. Inside, somebody, no doubt Zinty, was moving about. Davie thought for a moment of going in to say goodbye—but then he remembered Zinty's startled face in the Hall. He did not want to get involved in any amateur post-mortem. Besides it was close on six o'clock and it seemed to him that what he wanted more than anything was a pot of tea.

Davie always kept six teas in his pantry and greatly delighted in creating his own blend. This afternoon he felt in need of support. Neither Lapsang, nor Kee Mun, nor Oolong, nor Jasmine, was what he wanted, and certainly not Earl Grey. He brewed a pot of Darjeeling, adding three leaves from a jar of red bergamot, and brought it on a tray to a table by the window overlooking the Close. There were two novels on the table, *Death in September* and *The Last Will and Testament of Simon Cassidy*. Davie automatically put his hand out, paused, and withdrew it. What on earth was he thinking of? It was indecent. Then he took Brauer's testament from his pocket

and laid that beside the tray. He would open it presently. But not yet. Just at the moment he needed
music. Davie was the possessor of a very noble record
player. He put on the last side of *Ariadne auf Naxos.*

Against the music Davie did not hear a twice-re-
peated knock. He was surprised, therefore, when the
door opened quietly and revealed Zinty, pale-faced
and hesitant.

"Excuse me, I wanted very much to speak to you."

"Come in, my dear man," said Davie, "I'm just having some tea. Do join me. Sit down. But do just
listen to the end of this."

"I always think," said Davie when the music had
come to its splendid conclusion, "that you can write
music about Mediterranean gods and goddesses. I
don't know if it's because they're so beautiful, or
because we invest them with human attributes, but
to me they're entirely credible. Gods of the north,
on the other hand, and all those humourless super-
men with spears and targes and horns in their hair—
they're outside experience; I don't believe in them.
I don't just mean Wagner. You know all those other
boring works about Celtic Kings, and crusaders, and
Boadicea. There's no human interest in them. But
a Greek god, now—"

Davie was suddenly aware that Zinty was not listening.

"Please," Zinty said, "please . . . I have to tell
you something."

"I'm sorry. I babble so. Anything you want to say,
please say it. If I can help you at all—"

"You can't help me in any way, sir—except by
listening."

"I'll gladly listen."

"I thought I could do something and get away
with it," said Zinty. "Now I realize that I can't. It's
boiling inside me. I've got to get rid of it. I've got

to tell someone. I thought I'd be proud of my work —but I'm not! I'm ashamed of it. I wish I hadn't done it. Vengeance is all right for a god. Not for a man."

He stopped. Davie filled in the pause by passing him a cup of tea. It was strong and hot and sweet. It might, he thought, be useful. Zinty drank it and Davie watched him. He saw a tall brown man with bright blue eyes set in a wasted face. The hair short, American style. The cup clattered against the saucer as he put it down on the table.

"Well," said Davie, "what's this thing you've done?"

"I have murdered Dr. Brauer," said Zinty.

"You've murdered Dr. Brauer—how on earth—?"

"I would have expected you to ask 'why,' not 'how.' "

"Well then—why?"

"Because Brauer was a murderer. Dr. Davie—I'll tell you something you don't know. Brauer was a notorious member of the medical staff at Auschwitz."

"I did know it."

"You *did?*" said Zinty, amazed.

"Not till today. He told me himself this morning."

"He told you? Why?"

"I think because he felt he was in danger of being exposed. He wanted to talk to somebody, too."

Zinty gasped.

"How much did he tell you?"

"Not much, I suppose. We only had a short and rather disjointed conversation."

"Don't tell me," said Zinty. "I will tell you."

"Certainly."

"I wouldn't be alive now if I hadn't been trained as a doctor. Because of that I was used in the medical blocks at the camp. So many people have written about those things. I needn't describe what went on there. Fortunately I was young, not important enough to fill a proper medical post. I was an orderly. I never had to do anything I was ashamed of. But I was a witness. I can never forget the things that I saw. The man in charge of all this was Dr. Pavik."

Zinty looked up at Davie as much to say "You recognize the name." Davie nodded.

"Before the war I lived in a small town in Czechoslovakia near the Hungarian border. I was engaged to be married. Her name was Maria and she was the sister of a great friend of mine. The war ended that in a stroke. I was called up to the army and I never saw Maria again—except once. Before many days I was in a prison camp. Some time after by a strange piece of luck, my friend got sent to the same camp. We were together a long time."

As Zinty paused and wiped his face nervously with his handkerchief, Davie said, "Your friend was Mr. Krasner, I take it."

Zinty started.

"Krasner? Why should you say that?"

"You mentioned him at dinner on Friday."

"Maybe I did. Cannot I have had more than one friend in a prison camp? One needs them, God knows. No—not Krasner. Certainly not."

"I'm sorry," said Davie. "I presumed too much."

"But we couldn't stay together, my friend and I. After two years they sent me to Auschwitz. I filled all sorts of different jobs for months and then one day I was told I was to be a laboratory assistant. My work was in the background but I couldn't help sometimes seeing the men and women who were brought into the operating theaters. And one day a most terrible thing happened. I saw—"

Zinty passed his hand before his eyes.

"Do you feel you must tell me this?" said Davie. "Please don't if it's going to upset you."

"No—I've got to tell you. I saw—I saw Maria. I

had to go into the theater for something—and there she was, on the table. Ordinarily we all spent our time endeavouring to be inconspicuous—but I lost control of myself. I dashed forward. I tried to say something. I don't really know what happened. I was pushed out of the room. And I don't know what happened to her. I can guess."

"I've heard part of this story already," said Davie. "It was Dr. Brauer who was doing that operation."

Zinty stared at him. "I thought you understood what I was talking about," he said.

"I thought I did."

"Then why go on with this pretense of Dr. Brauer? Why don't you say Dr. Pavik and have done with it?"

"Dr. Pavik—?"

Davie half rose from his chair.

"Dr. Brauer *was* Dr. Pavik. Didn't you know?"

"No—I didn't. It never even occurred to me. I can't believe it."

"You must. Pavik wasn't pursued as some war criminals were, because he was supposed to be dead. But he'd only got away to America—as so many did. There weren't many people who'd have been able to recognize him. The people who met him usually died, you see. But I and my friend never gave up. We had found each other again in America, you understand. We felt sure he was alive, and at last after twenty years waiting I saw him at a lecture. I attended the whole course and watched him. I was certain. Then we decided to make this conference our opportunity. We had found out that he took those tablets. I studied their exact size and shape and made a similar one from aconite. Just one. Aconite causes depression of the heart, ending in death from syncope. In a man suffering already from disease I knew its effect would be immediate. I undertook to introduce it into Pavik's bottle of tablets. That first night I went to his rooms, but the outer door was locked. As I came down stairs I ran into a young man who was going into the ground-floor rooms—"

"Mostyn-Humphries."

"I was terribly afraid I'd given myself away. But he didn't make anything of it. Then I called again on Saturday morning at a time I guessed he'd be out."

"I met you coming away, didn't I?"

"Yes. His rooms were open because his—his—"

"Bed-maker."

"Bed-maker was there. I said I wanted to write a message. She let me. On the table was a bottle of tablets. I slipped my tablet in. It had seemed a wildly improbable chance—and it came off at the first attempt. Then we waited. No doubt he had another bottle on him. It might be days before that particular tablet got used. I hoped it might be. If he had taken it after a week's delay no one would have had a clue what had happened—but no—it had to be in public and before my eyes. Dr. Davie, I'm not the sort of man who can take that sort of thing."

"I don't understand why you haven't kept your own counsel. You must know—"

"I'm horrified to feel that I'm just a cold, disgusting, calculating murderer."

"Yes—but you must know that I can't keep this to myself. It's my duty to inform the police."

"I know it is. I want you to inform the police. I don't want to go on living. The only thing I wanted was that Pavik should die. But I'm sorry now that I had to be the one to kill him."

Davie's telephone was in a small anteroom that lay between the sitting room and the bedroom. He was not a minute away, but when he returned Zinty had disappeared. Davie pulled his door open. As he stepped out on to the landing he heard a sharp crack, apparently from the set below. He hurried downstairs. Zinty's door was still wide. The suitcase was still where he had seen it. There was no one in the room.

Davie crossed the carpet and opened the bedroom door. The man he had been talking to three minutes earlier lay sprawled on the bed. A revolver lay on the ground where it had fallen. It was horribly obvious that Zinty had shot himself. Or rather (Davie corrected himself) it was horribly obvious that he had been shot, and probably by himself. But the window was open.

IX

Chief Inspector Hodges turned the key in Zinty's door and followed Davie upstairs.

"There must be an autopsy, of course," he said. "But from what you've told me it's pretty clear that the man shot himself—*and* poisoned Dr. Brauer. May I use your telephone, sir?"

"Certainly."

"I must get on to Dr. Scobie."

Before Davie had finished taking a decanter and glasses out of a corner cupboard Hodges was back again.

"He'll be round at once. Of course I haven't had time to get abreast of all this—but he asked me to tell you that you were quite right about Dr. Brauer's bottle of tablets. There were six that were good and one that wasn't. He said it was important and that you'd know what he means—so I'll be grateful if you'll tell me."

Davie stared at him.

"If it means what I'm pretty sure it does mean—then that wretched man downstairs killed himself for nothing. There *was* only one tablet. Zinty meant to kill Brauer. He thought he'd killed Brauer. But if the tablet's still there he didn't kill Brauer. Brauer probably died a perfectly natural death after all."

"Maybe he did, Dr. Davie. But now there's a suspicion that he didn't, and I'll have to report the death to the coroner."

"What happens then?"

"He orders a post-mortem, and the county pathologist does it. At once—that's important."

"When do you get the result?"

"Depends. I wouldn't think the report on Dr. Brauer would be ready before Wednesday morning. In which case the inquest would be Thursday. *You'll* have to give evidence in the case of Dr. Zinty, sir."

"I shall hate that," said Davie. "When?"

"Friday, I expect. After the other one."

X

He had never felt less like going to bed. It had been nine o'clock before Scobie had gone, eleven o'clock before the body had been removed; and only then did Davie remember that he hadn't dined. He made tea. There was a tin of Bath Olivers. He still didn't feel like reading *Death in September*. He picked up Brauer's envelope and put it down again. He didn't want to tackle that either. It was stiflingly hot. The windows facing the Close were open, but the great green lawn lay dark under a curtain of cloud. Tomorrow would be wet. The clock struck twelve. Davie sat down and wrote a letter to a nephew in Australia. Then one to a friend in America. Then he made out checks for three bills. He had managed to divert his mind, but he still felt sufficiently awake to think he would stroll over to the porter's lodge and post his letters.

He crossed Baxter's Court, and then because he always took a childish pleasure in seeing his shadow on the cloister wall he decided to reach First Court by way of the undercroft. He got no farther than the Norman pillar. Long before his shadow had reached anywhere near the far wall another shadow passed across the cloister and disappeared into G staircase—or was it the Master's Lodge? The old question unfailingly arose each time.

For a few seconds Davie was almost scared. Then he realized the obvious fact. He had seen a person, not a shade. He walked on and turned right into First Court, feeling slightly annoyed. He liked his nonsensical monk and wasn't in a mood at all to be regaled with a mysterious stranger drifting about the college like an avenger in some Gothic novel. Especially as it was presumably Cowl, or perhaps that extraordinary Mostyn-Humphries returning from one of his fabled nocturnal adventures. It couldn't have been the Master: he was in London. Davie glanced at the windows. The ground floor (Mostyn-Humphries) was dark; so, alas, was the first floor; but in Cowl's room a light was burning. Cowl then. Davie posted his letters and returned to his rooms a little put out. He went to bed, made no attempt to read, and turned off the light. Brauer probably died a perfectly natural death after all. Yes, but now there were suspicions. If Zinty had failed maybe his friend Krasner had succeeded. And because of what Zinty had believed to be true there would now have to be a post-mortem on Brauer.

Davie stared at the dark ceiling and went over the events of that long day. Two men had told him the deepest secrets of their hearts, and he had seen both of them lie dead. Zinty alone in a bare college bedroom: Brauer in public, on a platform, surrounded—no, not surrounded—in the face of some two hundred people. The scene was clearly etched in his mind, like one of those busy Victorian pictures by Frith—Derby Day, or The Railway Station, everyone sharply identified. How could any of those men and women have had anything to do with it? None of them was really near him. All of them could establish their positions in the Hall by the witness of their neighbours—except perhaps those who were standing at the back, and they were the farthest away from the tragedy. Vorloff had been at the back, and Willow.

Then there had been the second slightly different tableau—the one he had seen when he opened the Combination Room door and stepped onto the dais. Miss Banbury had sat down, and it was Willow who was kneeling by Brauer. There was Miss Eggar, staring at the floor, with several bits of glass in her hand; Zinty's frightened face; Jump talking to the Master; Caldecott and Parkin standing quietly on the left side of the dais; on the other side Vorloff, almost behind the screen by the oriel window; Cowl standing alone beneath the picture of Bishop Allbottel, a sunbeam lending a more than usually knowing look to the eye of the college's founder; Junge and Catherine, below the dais, standing together, their eyes steadfastly looking at Geoffrey Willow.

To Davie, as he wandered on the borders of sleep, there came a vague feeling that there had been something out of place. Hadn't someone done something, said something, looked something, been somewhere, that didn't quite fit? He would probably remember in the morning, and Goodness knew it was nearly morning already. Dr. Davie fell into a heavy sleep.

But it was still not too late for night wanderers. At that hour, and with considerable difficulty, an unpracticed climber was leaving the college by the way that Mostyn-Humphries usually entered it. And another person, less encumbered, was returning quietly from Baxter's Court to a staircase in another part of the college.

The clock on the chapel tower struck two. The College of St. Nicholas, St. Anastasius, and the Magnificent Virgin Edwina, was at peace.

It began to rain.

Tuesday

I

Davie woke early; it was only six-thirty, but he was wide awake, and (as is usually Man's habit) the first thing that came into his head was the last thing he had put into it the night before. He turned the small question over in his mind. The scene on the dais. Cowl and Willow and the Master, and Parkin had reason to be there. Caldecott . . . well. But why was Miss Eggar being so officious over the broken glass? Fusspottiness? And why had Miss Banbury been so swift to play the part of hospital nurse? Motherliness? And Vorloff—he didn't seem to be contributing anything at all.

And then another question curled into his mind. Who opened the door on the dais during the lecture? And when Davie had gone through the cloisters to the Combination Room—why hadn't he run into the person who should have been escaping by the same door at almost the same time. They could only have missed each other by seconds. But he had met no one except, of course, Catherine and Junge at the foot of the Hall stairs.

He had never seen Catherine in slacks before—and how trim and boyish she had looked. In Davie's usual opinion no woman should be allowed to wear trousers, especially tight trousers, over the age of twenty —and surely no women over that age *would* wear them if they could ever be regaled by the sight of their own monstrous behinds. Mrs. Caldecott for instance. He had once seen her gardening, and a sobering sight it had been—quite sufficient justification for the small rumour that Caldecott was not entirely faithful to the person of Mrs. Caldecott. It seemed strange that these curious creatures should always prefer to be fashionable rather than pleasing. That pale lilac lipstick, for instance. Didn't they realize that it made them look like somebody recently raised from the dead? Or didn't they mind? And as for the new short skirt and those horrible knees—they were worse than Mrs. Caldecott's back view. And that reminded Davie of Caldecott's saucy remarks about Miss Marden at the cocktail party; and so, by way of three women, he found his thoughts back at the heart of his problem. He'd seen no one—but, come to think of it, the other person might not have escaped. He could have ducked into the Combination Room cloakroom, or he might boldly have walked on to the dais, unnoticed in the confusion, and left the Hall in the ordinary way with everyone else.

Inevitably Tuesday was going to be a day of waiting. At the moment it was raining hard. Davie got up and made his morning tea. Then he opened Brauer's long envelope. Inside was a short will. Except for one bequest Brauer had left everything to St. Nicholas's College, "where I have found peace."

There was also a letter.

> Dear Davie—
> I have just told you a great secret. I don't know if you can keep it. Perhaps after I'm dead it won't matter if you do or not.

Davie lowered the letter to his knee and looked out at the driving rain. He *had* kept what might be the main part of Brauer's secret—the part that Brauer didn't even know that he knew. He had told Hodges most of Zinty's story—at the time that had seemed

essential—but he had not mentioned Zinty's identifi-
cation of Brauer with Pavik. That might not be true
(surely it couldn't be true?). And Zinty was dead.

Davie went on reading.

You will see that I have left you my Boys Playing Marbles, and my favourite Rockingham Cow.
I especially want you to have them in memory
of a friendship I have greatly valued. Please take
possession of them right away.

The rest of my collection I have left to the college. You were looking at those club glasses just
now. I don't want the college to be fooled, so I
must tell you that I have decided that they are
fakes. I don't think I have ever been duped before. I didn't get them at an auction or from a
usual dealer. A man in a small way of business
wrote to me about them. His name is Stumpf
and he has a queer little place (queer in every
sense) in Darnay Street, a little road off Great
Russell Street.

Stumpf? thought Davie. Stumpf? That was one of
the names in Brauer's doodle on the blotting paper.
And then he recalled how Brauer had looked at the
end of their interview that Monday. There had been
a lot more to tell—"a packet more." Would it have
been about Stumpf and that other character, Born?
To have found their way into that desperate doodling
Stumpf and Born must have had a very great significance for Brauer alive. With Brauer dead it was
impossible to know if they were still important in
his story.

I hope my affairs will not give you too much
trouble.

Yours—I was going to write "ever," but that won't
make sense by the time you get this—
So—

                              Yours affectionately,
                              Paul Brauer

Davie put the letter back with the will in the long
envelope. The chapel clock struck eight. The Master
wouldn't be back from London till about ten-thirty.
It would be Davie's duty to give him an account of
what had happened, but there were two and a half
hours to wait. Davie looked out of the window. The
rain had stopped. Everything was shining in the sun.
He decided to take an early walk to King's.

There was no one about. Even Mr. Jump at the
porter's lodge was still concealed in some distant re-
cess. So Davie traversed the Long Walk unseen, and
turned right into St. Nicholas Lane, stretching before
him almost as peaceful and empty as it might have
been a hundred years before. Mr. Saintly, the smart
barber, was taking an early breath on the steps of his
exclusive little shop. A postman passed along Sidney
Street. Before the grim facade of Whewell's Court
two bed-makers were exchanging morning remarks
about the weather. "The rain," they decided, "would
freshen everything up."

Davie dived into All Saints Passage and at the
other end turned left into Trinity Street. A taxi
was standing in front of the Blue Boar. As Davie
approached, two men walked quickly out of the hotel
and got into it. They were Bondini and Colonel Vorloff. "Stopped over," said Davie to himself. "It was
civil of them not to stay in college." But now his
mind was back with the conference and Zinty, and he
no longer wanted to go for an early walk. At the
end of Trinity Street he turned down into the silent
Market Place and made for home. He would go

back to the Lodge, he thought, take a turn in the garden and wait for the Master in his study. And, as it happened, it was the right thing to do. The Master, surprisingly, was already there.

"The dinner ended earlier than I'd feared. So I came back on what the junior members of the university call the Fornicator."

"I have always thought the name a strange one," said Davie demurely. "The train is guiltless. We have here a classic example both of the transferred epithet and of the pathetic fallacy."

"I wonder when the name started. An Edwardian joke?"

"I'm not so sure. Engines have names like Rob Roy and The Dover Castle. The Cambridge Fornicator," said Davie solemnly, "is a name better fitted to the stagecoach. It's pleasant to think of it in the age of Pickwick starting out each evening from Snow Hill."

"But even then an example of the transferred epithet."

"Certainly—but being pre-Ruskin not of course an example of the pathetic fallacy."

"If you'll develop that in a brief thesis," said the Master, "I think we will be able to award you a Ph.D. And now will you have the goodness to tell me the news; I'm sure you've got plenty."

"I certainly have," said Davie, sinking into an armchair.

II

"Well," said Dr. Courtney, "if the Zinty confession turns out to be an enormous mistake—as you rather think it will—we're exactly where we were."

"Not quite. There's his friend. Zinty blazed up at me when I presumed that the friend of the conspiracy was Krasner. But I would think that that was only to protect Krasner. He'd said too much. But if I was right and the fellow conspirator *was* Krasner, then he may have followed an alternate plan."

"He wouldn't have used it if he had supposed that the first plan had succeeded."

"Ah—but time was running out. If Krasner had a plan—and I think he must have had one—he might have decided not to wait any longer."

"If the friend was *not* Krasner you don't even know that he was in Cambridge."

"That's true."

"It's quite important."

Mrs. Courtney entered the study bearing two cups of coffee.

"It all seems highly improbable to me," the Master was saying, "but if the post-mortem does reveal a murder—we're talking about poor Brauer, Adela: it seems there's trouble."

"That doesn't surprise me in the least," said Mrs. Courtney. "All that talk on Sunday afternoon about poisons. There couldn't have been anything else but trouble."

"I was saying—*if*—then Krasner, I suppose, is the first suspect. Who else could have had it in for Brauer? Quiet, harmless, well-liked by a number of discerning people."

"Really, Clive!" said Mrs. Courtney. "You are the most simple of men—don't you agree, Dr. Davie?— Mr. Cowl never liked him, I know; then there's Dr. Caldecott—ambition: Geoffrey Willow—ambition. And from something he said I think Colonel Vorloff wasn't much in favour. There's four for a start."

"Merciful Powers!" said the Master.

* * *

Davie let himself out by the cloister door and turned into G staircase. He wanted to fulfill Brauer's wish to secure Boys Playing Marbles and the Rockingham Cow before Mrs. Pilsworthy had attained her long-deferred ambition to tidy up. But the first thing he saw as he mounted the stairs was not the outer oak of Brauer's rooms, but the bent posterior of Mrs. Pilsworthy herself, who was apparently endeavouring to peer through its large keyhole. And Davie was immediately to learn that Mrs. Pilsworthy had been prevented from undertaking her dangerous mission by the unexplained loss of the key.

Keys to the sets hung from a board in the porter's lodge and every bed-maker knew precisely where the keys belonging to her staircase were, but this morning, when she had called at the lodge this key had been missing. "You could have knocked me down with a feather," said Mrs. Pilsworthy. "Never in all my service at the college, sir, has one of my keys been out of place. It did happen once, I remember, to Mrs. Tarrant on Q, but never on G, sir. 'Well, Mr. Jump,' I said, 'I put it back myself yesterday morning,' I said, 'and that I know. If anyone has moved it, that person had better find it,' I said."

"Well, fortunately, I have a key, Mrs. Pilsworthy," said Davie. "But actually at the moment I think it will be best if we leave the room undisturbed. I am Dr. Brauer's executor and will have to examine everything just as he left it. You understand."

"Very well, sir," said Mrs. Pilsworthy, "if such is your wish, sir, so it shall be."

"Thank you, Mrs. Pilsworthy."

And Mrs. Pilsworthy continued upstairs, breathing heavily, and in prime condition to do a violence to the first frangible object she might find in Cowl's rooms.

Davie let himself in and noted with pleasure that

the Boys were still safely engaged in their game and the Cow still watching from her position on the bookcase. He looked about him for a minute and then entered the bedroom and crossed to the small window that looked down on the cloister. He was standing there thinking more about the humours of Mrs. Pilsworthy than the tragedy of his dead friend when a gentle creak in the room he had just left cut across his thoughts. Davie tiptoed to the half-open door and peered through the crack by the hinges. It was Cowl.

"Hullo!" said Davie, opening the door and stepping into the room. "What brings you here?"

"The oak," said Cowl. "It was open. I thought I ought to have a look. I was curious, too. I haven't been in this room for years. I wanted to look at the famous collection. I admit I used to wonder if he really did know. Beastly of me. Look at that Meissen Europa and the Bull. Glorious. What brings *you* here?"

"I'm Brauer's executor."

"Well, I'd better leave you to it. Or," he added, turning round in the doorway, "I'll help you if I can be of any assistance."

"Thanks very much, Cowl, but I think I can manage."

Cowl nodded and turned to leave.

"Have they decided what hit him?" he said, pausing with his hand on the door-knob.

"I haven't heard anything to disturb the supposition that it was a thrombosis."

"H'm," said Cowl. "I just wondered."

III

Davie placed the Boys in one pocket and the Cow in the other, and locked the door. It was odd about the bed-maker's key and before going back to his rooms Davie called at the porter's lodge.

"What can have happened to it, Mr. Jump?"

"I'm sure I have no idea, sir. The responsibility is Mrs. Pilsworthy's."

"I don't know how it can be that, Mr. Jump. When she leaves it here it leaves her custody."

"Ah . . . but did she leave it here?" said Mr. Jump darkly.

"I must say," said Davie, "now I think of it, it's all a bit precarious. If you happened to be at the back of your office, or even if your attention were diverted for a moment, anyone *could* lift a key without difficulty. What by the way is *that?*" And Davie pointed to a key that was lying lightly shoved under some papers on the corner of Mr. Jump's counter nearest the door.

Mr. Jump examined the key.

"That's the key," said Mr. Jump, blushing slightly. "Just as I thought. Mrs. Pilsworthy must have put it down there yesterday morning. A lot of fuss about nothing. These bed-makers—"

"It's found, that's the great thing," said Davie, and set off to return to Baxter's Court.

Back in his rooms he placed the two pieces of china in the positions to which they had long been accustomed, the Boys on the chimney-piece and the Cow on a nearby bookcase.

"Cold Pastoral!" quoted Davie,

"When old age shall this generation waste,

Thou shalt remain,"
—provided, of course, that what Mrs. Pilsworthy and
Time had spared were not consumed by the atten-
tions of his own bed-maker, Mrs. Tibbs. He would
have to speak to her about that tomorrow. And he
knew very well what Mrs. Tibbs would say. "I am
sure, Dr. Davie, you have had no cause to complain
of damages since I have been on this staircase. Careful I have always been. Too careful, my poor husband always said." And then he would have to say
that never had he had better service than that ren-
dered by Mrs. Tibbs but he had thought that he
ought to draw her attention to the new pieces. And
then Mrs. Tibbs would say that he had made her
quite nervous. And he would finally get it out: "Just
leave them alone, Mrs. Tibbs. I'd rather they were
my responsibility. Then it'd be nobody's fault but
mine." And "As you wish, I'm sure, Dr. Davie," Mrs.
Tibbs would say, and would conduct herself with
considerable dignity for the next twenty-four hours.
Mrs. Tibbs was as prickly as Mrs. Pilsworthy about
anything that encroached upon her mystery.

Davie looked at his watch. It was still only half-
past ten. A long day stretched ahead, filled with
doubts and uncertainties.

IV

Not long before the Boys and the Rockingham
Cow had been installed in their new home, the Cambridge nine o'clock train had slid impressively into
Liverpool Street station. Now, after four minutes'
bustle, the platform was empty again, except for
three porters working on the luggage van, and a
cleaner, who was cheerfully engaged in collecting

abandoned newspapers, sweeping out cigarette cartons, and occasionally salvaging a lost glove or a lonely umbrella.

Ada Trott was not one of those cleaners who combine a dirty job with Bond Street manners. She did not wear earrings. Her hair was not bleached. She did not use lipstick or nail varnish. She was a stout party with grizzled hair, red cheeks, a knob of a nose, and eyes like an owl behind thick glasses. She wore a gold ring on her left hand and she was the mother of four grown-up children.

Ada went along the train opening and banging doors, and as she went she sang aloud to herself "The Lily of Laguna," which she had heard on the previous night in an old-time radio program. She thought the old tunes were very much pleasanter than those noisy things you usually heard nowadays. "She's my Lily of Laguna," sang Ada, opening the last door but one, "she's my lily and—" And there in the middle of the line she stopped.

A cleaner with bleached hair and red fingernails would probably have screamed. Ada was made of stronger stuff. She entered the carriage and touched the body that lay on the floor. "Oh my goodness!" said Ada. Then she bundled out again and set off down the platform as fast as her fat legs would carry her.

"Hi, Ada!" a porter called by the luggage van. "You ain't working to rule this morning."

Ada said nothing. She wasn't going to ask help from stupid Joe Bancock. She wanted Mr. Southcombe the ticket collector. And fortunately there he was, just moving away from the gate, talking to Mr. Dinsbury.

Wednesday

I

At ten o'clock on Wednesday morning Davie received a telephone call from the Lodge. Inspector Hodges had been calling on the Master and he now had questions to put to Davie: might he come across?

"I take it," said Davie as Hodges entered his room attended by a satellite constable, "I take it that Dr. Brauer did not die a natural death."

"I don't know why you should take it, sir—"

"Thy face bewrayeth thee," said Davie.

"Well—you're right, sir. He didn't. He was poisoned."

"Poisoned—and not by Zinty."

"No, sir—and not in the way you'd expect either. He didn't take poison by the mouth. He died from an injection of poison into the bloodstream."

Hodges paused impressively.

"You see what that means, Dr. Davie."

"It means there were two separate attempts to kill him."

"Yes. There was poison in the tablet, but not in the stomach—and the poison that killed Dr. Brauer was not the same as the poison in the tablet. The poison in the tablet was just what Zinty said it was —aconite. It appears that Dr. Brauer must have been attacked by much the same kind of method as that used by savages—you know—the blow-pipe sort of thing. The poison is quick. The victim dies almost at once. . . . You see the difficulty, sir?"

"I do, indeed, Inspector. If Brauer was injected it

must have been on the platform in full sight of everybody in the audience—which seems highly improbable."

"But if Dr. Moberly's facts are right, inescapable."

"And the inquest is when?" asked Davie.

"Tomorrow morning."

"I hope I don't have to give evidence."

"No, sir. Dr. Courtney will identify the body. After that there'll be the medical evidence—and then almost certainly an adjournment. You won't be troubled at all. The other one's on Friday morning."

Davie stood looking out of the window. Then, "Did Dr. Moberly find the wound?" he asked "—The puncture or whatever it would be?"

"Certainly. In the back of the neck, a bit to the right. It wasn't the broken glass did it. And the queer question is how could it have been done in those circumstances? He wasn't even hit in a part of his body that was facing the audience."

"Ah . . . but wait a minute. There may be an explanation of that. I've just remembered."

Davie told the inspector about the opening of the Combination Room door immediately before Brauer's collapse.

"That's certainly interesting," said Hodges.

"And another thing—one can't help wondering. I'm afraid it sounds a little too spectacular—a little too theatrical—"

"What does, sir?"

"I was going to say one can't help wondering if that theft at the Missionary Exhibition had anything to do with it. A blow-pipe is stolen—and two days later a man is killed. . . ."

II

Miss Ramble had almost nothing to tell—but she made the most of a precious opportunity.

"So good of you to call, Inspector," she said. "I know how busy you always are, and how small my own little trouble must seem to you, but it is very distressing to me, I assure you, for all the objects in the exhibition have been lent by Headquarters, and poor Miss Ramble has to account for them. Normally, Inspector, the room is never unattended. When I run out for my lunch interval, or for my quarter of an hour at teatime, my friend, Miss Ogle, takes my place, but on Saturday she complained of a headache and I advised her strongly to return home after luncheon. As it happened it proved to be a very busy afternoon with several conference visitors from St. Nicholas's College: which I must say pleased me very much—it was so kind of Dr. Willow to include our handbill. Well, Inspector, I had necessarily intended to forego my tea, but at about five-fifteen who should come in but Mrs. Courtney and the children—on a second visit. I told her about Miss Ogle, and she said 'But you must have your tea, Miss Ramble. The children are determined to inspect all those terrible weapons of yours again, and I'm sure I won't get them away for at least twenty minutes.' Well, unfortunately, Inspector, I was detained. I met a dear old friend of mine at the Cosy Pantry and I'm afraid it must have been more like twenty-five minutes before I got back. Mrs. Courtney and the children were still there but left as soon as I arrived. I did not notice anything was wrong till just before six, when the exhibition closes—and then, to my dismay, I discovered that the glass case containing the weapons had been broken, and that the smallest of the blow-pipes was missing. I communicated with the police at once, and telephoned to Mrs. Courtney. She told me that no one had visited the exhibition while she was present, but that she had left the children for five minutes while she went to a neighbouring shop, and that during that interval she understood there had been one visitor, but the children had not known who he was. He had not stayed long and the children had gone out of the room and waited for their mother on the landing. It was hardly looking after the room in my absence, I must say. It does look as if this man must have been responsible for the abstraction—but I have no idea who he may have been. One of your men very kindly studied the case for fingerprints, but it was such a popular exhibit, especially with children, that it probably had hundreds—or now I come to think of it, none at all, for I always go round with a duster morning and night, and it was when I was rubbing the case that I discovered the loss."

"Most of these blow-pipes are pretty long," said Hodges. "That one's about six foot. You couldn't conceal it."

"They are not all so big," said Miss Ramble. "That one is shorter, and the missing one was more the size of a flute. Perhaps they use it in the jungle where a large pipe would be difficult to maneuver, or for close quarters."

"Close quarters," said Hodges. "I daresay you're right."

III

The Courtney children were as reticent as Miss Ramble had been loquacious. Very pink in the face, Clarissa told the inspector that the man had been very tall, and Richard said he looked "awful." Abel at first refused to answer.

"Did he say anything?" asked Hodges.

Clarissa and Richard looked at each other as though so difficult an enquiry required combined consideration. Then Richard said, "No, he didn't," and Clarissa added, "Not a word. He just gave us a look."

"He was very ugly," said Abel suddenly.

"Be quiet, Abel," muttered Richard.

"He was," said Abel. "Uglier than anybody that ever was."

"And so we went outside," said Clarissa, "and waited till Mother came back."

"You must have seen the man when he came out. How soon was that?"

"Almost at once," said Richard. "He came out quickly and went downstairs fast."

"Would you recognize him if you saw him again?"

"I don't—" began Clarissa, but Richard said, "I would."

"So would I," said Abel. "He was the ugliest man in the whole world."

IV

Hodges had arranged with Davie to meet in the Hall as soon as he had finished talking with the children.

"It doesn't get us very far," he said. "A man. No one saw him except the children, and children are not reliable when it comes to description. What's 'very tall' to them may be quite an ordinary height. Now, sir—show me. You were in the gallery and you saw the top of the door opening—but you didn't actually see anybody."

"No, the screens were in the way."

"Here and here about?"

"Yes."

"But you feel sure somebody did come in because of the way Dr. Brauer looked in that direction?"

"Yes. It was unmistakable."

"Who could have come that way?"

"Thousands *could* have. We can only be sure of those who were in the room—and no one person—except, perhaps, Dr. Willow—could remember all of them."

"Well—someone or other opens that door. And standing about here he shoots at Dr. Brauer. A small dart wouldn't disappear. It should have been found."

"You've been over the dais?"

"Every inch."

"Someone must have retrieved it."

"Whoever it was had a twenty-four-hour start."

"I would imagine a murderer would have tried to accomplish that necessary act as soon as possible. There were a number of people on the platform after Brauer fell."

"Do you remember who, sir?"

"Let me see—the Master, Mr. Cowl, and Dr. Caldecott, Dr. Parkin—at least two others—and Miss Banbury and Miss Eggar. I suppose they were all in the front row. Then Dr. Willow pushed forward. Miss Banbury was holding Dr. Brauer's head against her knee. By the time I got round to the dais Colonel Vorloff had joined them."

"They don't sound very likely murderers—except the foreign chap—Vorloff? Who's he?"

"A distinguished author and explorer."

"H'm—the weapon could have been recovered later."

"Or do you think it could have been recovered not by the murderer but by an accomplice?"

"I don't see any of those people a murderer, sir, and at first thought it isn't easy to see them as an accomplice either."

"Yes—but I can't help feeling that one of them may have been," said Davie.

"Let us go over this again. Someone comes in quietly through this door. Dr. Brauer sees him. The man fires and gets away through the door. And unless he comes back later what he fired will have to be collected by an accomplice. Is that right so far?"

"No, Inspector. I've just thought of something. Two things. Brauer didn't show alarm when he saw the person. Only annoyance. I'm sure *he* didn't think the person was a likely assailant. I think he knew whoever it was."

"And the other point, sir?"

"You say Brauer was shot in the back of the neck, a little to the right. How do you hit a man there if you're standing to his left?"

"You can't."

"Unless he turns round."

"And did he?"

"Certainly—but the wrong way. He turned sharply and looked at the person. It's not a constructive observation, I'm afraid, but I'm quite sure Brauer never presented his whole back to the person in the wings."

"It could have been the accomplice who was by the door. There were screens on the other side. Couldn't Dr. Brauer have been shot from there?"

"He could, except for these reasons. Whoever it was would have had to conceal himself there long before anyone entered the Hall, and would have risked being discovered. Second, there was no escape: there's no door that side. I can't imagine anyone choosing to operate from that side, if he could operate from the other."

"And the window?"

"Doesn't open. It's for light not air."

"H'm . . . then in spite of your belief, sir, that Dr. Brauer did not turn his back on the other side, I can't help feeling that momentarily he must have done so. Where was he standing in relation to the lectern?"

"A little to the lectern's right."

"And the lectern was in the center?"

"Yes—about here."

"That puts him on the window side of the dais."

"Yes."

"What hand did he use to pick up the glass?"

Dr. Davie considered.

"It was in his right hand when he drank it."

"Then, sir, he may have turned a certain extent at that moment."

"A certain extent—yes."

"He wouldn't have to turn very far to expose a point just right of the center of his neck."

"No—I suppose you're right. It is possible."

Inspector Hodges looked pleased. He valued Dr.

Davie's help and advice, but he had no notion of his being in the right about everything.

"I haven't asked you," he said, "if Dr. Brauer had any enemies."

"If Zinty's story is true, he certainly had. But I can tell you this for certain—he didn't make enemies here. He was quiet—kept very much to himself. Some people, I think, were envious of him. For my part I liked him. He was a lonely sort of chap. He'd lost his home and his past and he'd sunk new roots with us. He had an affection for the college—and that pleased me."

Davie knew that he ought to mention Dr. Pavik. He couldn't bring himself to do so.

"Well—thank you, sir, for your help. And please let me know if anything strikes you further. I've got a devil of a job tracing all these people. Of course the non-Cambridge people got away before there was any mention of murder."

"Dr. Willow could tell you most of their addresses, I think."

"It's the people in the front rows that are most important. If there was anything to see, one of them ought to have seen it."

"Except of course that many of them were ancient Cambridge worthies, probably half asleep. They had reserved seats and Willow must have had a plan. I'll ask him, shall I?"

"I wish you would, sir. I'm going to call there a little later. Perhaps he'd have the information ready for me."

V

Five minutes later Davie opened the door of Willow's house in St. Nicholas Lane and let himself in. Geoffrey Willow was in his study. From the drawing room upstairs came the sound of a dark contralto voice, practicing.

"I'm afraid I'm a nuisance," said Davie, "but I wondered—could you tell me who were sitting in the front two rows at Brauer's lecture?"

"Well—the front row I could. Why d'you want to know?"

"Inspector Hodges asked me to find out. The postmortem has discovered trouble, and there'll have to be an inquest. They want witnesses."

"I see. Well . . . there were reserved seats for the Master and Mrs. Courtney, Caldecott and Parkin, old Manners, and Dr. and Mrs. Finn—that's all. The rest were free for first-comers. Miss Banbury was one of the first people in the Hall and sat down in the middle of the front row. Miss Eggar came in much later but was very determined to get to the front. She pushed her way through and sat down near the left end of the front row; that's nine. And Cowl ten."

"Odd that he came at all."

"Yes—but Cowl's odd about everything. He was sitting by Miss Eggar. I don't remember who was in the second row—probably not people I know."

"Perhaps Catherine would know," said Davie, glancing at the ceiling.

"Catherine wasn't there."

"I remember now—I met her outside the Hall. She's a funny girl—after taking all that trouble with the dais."

"She did that for me and the conference. But she absolutely refused—so she said—to sit down and listen to Brauer's triumphant progress towards the professorship. Nothing would induce her. So she came to the college and did a lot of work for me in the conference office."

"You've got a devoted wife, Geoffrey."

"That's what wives are for," said Willow.

VI

When Davie got back to his rooms he sat down at his table and wrote the following notes.

1. Brauer seems to have been killed by something like a poisoned dart.

2. A blow-pipe was stolen from the exhibition two days before. This is an extraordinary coincidence.

3. Who was the person behind the screen? Could anyone have got there by mistake? If not by mistake why else would the person be there? I still don't think the person was in a position to hit Brauer in the back of the neck. Why were the screens there anyhow? Many important lectures have been given from that dais, but I never saw it dolled up like that before. Another coincidence? It was Catherine's idea.

4. If a dart was fired it ought to have been found. It wasn't.

5. Could such a dart be fired and not seen at the time of firing?

6. There have been two attempts to kill Brauer, one successful, one unsuccessful. Does that mean two murderers? If two, does it mean two in league or two independent ones?

Davie read his notes over and drew a firm line underneath them. Then he went to the telephone and asked the Courtney children to tea.

VII

Davie's bedder, Mrs. Tibbs, had finished her work and was ready to leave. The last two days had provided her many opportunities for reflecting on the shortness of life and the sadness of Dr. Brauer's sudden departure—which, oddly enough, had closely resembled the end of a cousin of her husband's, Mr. Wagpole, a very nice man, who had collapsed quite unexpectedly at a dinner given by the Ancient Order of Buffaloes. But just now Mrs. Tibbs could think of nothing better than to remark upon the progress of work on the oriel window. Standing at the back window of Davie's rooms and looking across the court at the white-aproned figure on the scaffolding, she observed that Mr. Wilkins had been a good six weeks at the old window without a break and she'd like to know when he'd finish it.

"Not quite without a break, Mrs. Tibbs," said Davie. "It was wet yesterday and he had to knock off on Monday because of the lecture—"

"Excuse me, sir," said Mrs. Tibbs, "but that he never. I saw him with my own eyes. I'd come in early that afternoon, sir—I like a bustle I will not deny, and I come in different from my usual because I thought I'd like to see all the people coming out of the lecture. I was up here doing a little tidying, and I come to the back window to shake out my duster. 'O!' I says to myself, 'There's Mr. Wilkins. I hope he isn't going to interrupt the lecture with his old clink-clink,' I says; and just as though he might have heard me saying it, he turns round and nips down the ladder and goes into the little shed below."

"He must have forgotten, Mrs. Tibbs, and come down as soon as he realized his mistake."

"He didn't hang around, sir, Mr. Wilkins didn't. He was out of his shed in no time and off through the arch. There never was a man like Mr. Wilkins for being in a hurry. I had to laugh. If he'd remembered the old lecture he wouldn't have been late for something else. More haste less speed, as my poor husband always used to say."

As Davie passed through the court on his afternoon stroll he made a point of pausing by the scaffolding and asking Wilkins how he was getting on. Mr. Wilkins replied that he would get along a lot quicker if people left him and his work alone. "Not meaning you, sir. I mean meddlers. I wasn't here Monday, as you know, and Tuesday it was raining. And what do I find? First of all my overalls with the arms pulled inside out and hanging where I didn't leave them. Now that's cheek to begin with!"

"It certainly is."

"And, second, someone's been fooling about on my scaffolding."

"I'm sorry about that," said Davie. "Some ass went up there on Sunday night and put a ban-the-bomb flag on two of the poles."

"Beats me," said Mr. Wilkins. "In term time you expect undergraduates to climb up any scaffolding they find. It's got a sort of fascination for them. But in the long vacation when there's only a few scholars about, you'd have thought they'd have known betterer than that. Besides, sticking flags in one thing, but there's a small diamond pane cut out of the window—"

"*What?*" said Davie.

"True, sir. Someone's cut a bit of glass out clean as a whistle. And the queer thing is it's been put back again."

Davie climbed up the ladder. It was perfectly true. A diamond pane, near the bottom of the window—at shoulder height as he stood on the platform about a foot below the sill—had been taken from the leads —and put back carefully, but not carefully enough.

"That's a most extraordinary thing, Wilkins. Have you told the Bursar?"

"No, sir. The job I was on Monday kept me over Tuesday, so I only found it today, or of course I'd have let Dr. Willow know at once. Matter of fact I only noticed it half an hour back."

Dr. Davie returned to earth, his heart beating with excitement. He would have enjoyed keeping his discovery to himself in the manner of the traditional private detective, but as he knew he could not do that he took himself off to the police station, turning the new addition to the story over and over in his mind as he walked.

"Brauer was hit by something. I knew it wasn't from the Combination Room side. But it didn't seem possible for it to come from the window. Now it's plain that it could have done. Mrs. Tibbs saw someone on the scaffolding at the time of the attack on Brauer, someone who'd taken the trouble to disguise himself as Wilkins. The pane must have been removed on Sunday night. There were two, then, on the scaffolding that night. The chap with the banner, and someone else. No one would have noticed a complete pane missing. If they had, they'd have thought it was part of the repair work. It must have been put back on Monday night. A risk—but putting it back was an essential part of the trick. Now does that link up with the missing weapon and the man the children saw? It ought to—but for one thing. If you're going to commit a murder in that way, surely you'd come ready equipped, not trust to the lucky chance of finding what you wanted at a temporary exhibition. . . . On the other hand if the thing were sudden, not premeditated . . . a man in a state of unexpected indignation might accept an idea accidentally put in his way. Even then he'd have to have brought the poison. That wasn't at the exhibition. The only thing one can be sure of now is that it *could* have been done from the outside—when Brauer turned to look to his left. But we're no nearer knowing who it was that made him do that. There must have been two—one on the scaffold, one behind the screen on the other side. Maybe three if one of them was in the audience."

Halfway along St. Nicholas Lane Davie passed Baggs and Mostyn-Humphries; and Davie had a sudden thought.

"Ah—Baggs," he said, turning on his heel.

"Afternoon, sir."

"Baggs—I understand that on Monday morning an injunction inscribed in red characters upon a rather grubby piece of linen, and bearing some reference to the banning of something or other, was discovered to have been affixed with singular impropriety to the scaffolding surrounding the oriel window. I have given some thought to this matter and have been driven to the unwelcome conclusion that this puerile and curiously ineffectual escapade could hardly have been devised by anyone but yourself. Am I right?"

"Er—yes, Dr. Davie, I did do it."

"I thought so."

"I put it up because I thought I ought to have a bang—have a go—at doing something to impress all these foreign visitors."

"I doubt very much if any of them saw it, Baggs, and I am quite sure that they wouldn't have been the least impressed if they had. At what time of night did you contrive this remarkable gesture?"

"About one o'clock, sir."

"You'd have been much better asleep. But tell me —this may seem an odd question, but it has some importance in view of the two tragedies which have occurred—did you see any sign of anyone else having been on the scaffolding?"

"No—no I didn't. I was in too much of a hurry."

"Yes, of course. Well—don't waste your talents, Baggs—it's a great mistake."

And Davie passed on his way towards Police Headquarters.

"But my beautiful Baggs," said Mostyn-Humphries, "what was the point in saying you put that awful thing up at one o'clock?"

"Because I did."

"You did not. I saw you as a matter of fact—just after I'd climbed in. And that was about a quarter past two. And there you were just hopping down the scaffolding."

"I was not."

Mostyn-Humphries stopped dead.

"I saw someone there at two-fifteen."

"Well that was what old Davie wanted to know, you silly clod. You ought to tell him."

"Perhaps I will. And I will thank you, Baggs, not to address me as clod. As I have often remarked—"

"Oh stow it," said Baggs.

VIII

Hodges was looking very pleased with himself. There was a smile playing round the corner of his mouth which seemed to say "No matter what you have to tell me, it won't be equal to what I have to tell you." In the end it proved an even balance. It looked as though Davie had found out how the crime had been committed. It looked as though Hodges had found the weapon, or one part of the weapon, the blow-pipe. "It was hidden under the sand in a council bin on the side of St. Nicholas Lane," he said. "Criminals usually make mistakes—but this was a wildly silly one. The thing might have been hidden for a week or two, but it had to be discovered in time. As it turned out it was discovered in two days. The labourer who found it reads his local paper. Naturally he didn't connect it with the death of Dr. Brauer—but he did remember the theft from the exhibition. He took it to Miss Ramble and Miss Ramble informed us."

"Fingerprints?" said Davie.

"Miss Ramble's and the workman's."

"Yes, of course; that would be the trouble."

"And some others."

Hodges did not disdain the dramatic climax.

"Well?"

"The others are too smudged to show anything certain—but the strange thing about them is that they don't belong to the hands of a very tall man. If they are a man's they're a very small man's. They're more like a woman's."

Davie whistled.

"Strange it is, sir. But we'll discover what it means. We've gone a long way. We're looking for a small-made man—"

"Or perhaps a woman," said Davie in a half-whisper.

"Or perhaps a woman, who was on that scaffold at twenty to four on Monday—and it isn't often in a case of this sort one can start from anything as precise as that."

"I must be getting back," said Davie. "The Courtney children are coming to tea."

"See what you can get out of them about that man, please. And one other thing—how big is this Mr. Wilkins? Is he a big man, as the children said?"

"Wilkins is rather a small man."

"H'm—well, as I've said before, I don't think much of children's measurements. There's another point, too. If the pane of glass was put back on Monday night then the person who did it must have remained in Cambridge."

"I daresay several did. It might have been inconvenient to leave suddenly. Vorloff, I know, stayed at the Blue Boar. So did Bondini. I saw them, quite by accident, leaving on Tuesday morning. You can check on the hotels."

"That is being done," said Hodges with just a shade of dignity.

"Of course," said Davie quickly.

Then he had to put his foot in it again. "It occurs to me, Inspector, that you ought to find out if anyone had bought a diamond. No one would have arrived glass-cutter in pocket."

"No, sir; but perhaps you don't know you can do that sort of thing with a ring."

"No, I didn't know that," said Davie, slightly abashed.

"And a leaded glass, which I suppose this was, you can prise out with a penknife."

"Yes, it was."

"There's one thing I don't like about this already," Hodges went on. "Wasn't it taking an extravagant risk doing it that way, through the window? Couldn't he have done the job another time of day or night, and done it easier in another place?"

Davie recovered his confidence.

"No—I don't agree. It was a very good way. At any other time or place there was a danger of being seen. At that time and place there was practically none. Indeed he—or she—would *not* have been seen if it hadn't been for Mrs. Tibbs's inordinate affection for social gatherings. And after the thing had been fired—or whatever the word is for using a blow-pipe—the person could have nipped up the Hall stairs and been at the back of the meeting in less than a minute."

"Two," said Hodges. "You're making it too smart."

"Two then. Any of the people at the back when Brauer fell may really have been there only a few seconds. No one would have noticed—especially if the person was familiar, someone who might reasonably have been there anyhow."

"You're quite a theorist, Dr. Davie," said Hodges.

Davie got up. "You must forgive my amateur speculations. My mind runs on."

"You have been very helpful, sir. I'll be round in about ten minutes to look at that window and the scaffolding. But we've lost two days there—"

"And it rained buckets on Monday night."

"No chance of footprints. But the shed might have something. And I must talk to Mrs. What's-it."

"Tibbs. She won't be in college now. But she lives quite near, somewhere off King Street. The porter will tell you."

IX

On the way home Davie decided to call again on the Willows. Geoffrey was out, but Catherine was upstairs in the first-floor drawing room. She was practicing scales. Davie waited outside the door till she came to a resting place. Then he tapped on the door and entered. She was seated at the piano, and wearing the tight trousers that she had boldly worn in college on Monday. Automatically Davie had a vision of Mrs. Caldecott gardening.

"Dr. Davie!" Catherine got up with open arms. Davie gave her a bachelor's kiss.

"Why this honor?"

"I wanted to ask you to be good enough to answer a question or two."

"Certainly—but why?"

"There's some trouble about poor Brauer. There's got to be an inquest and the police asked me to find out one or two things for them."

"Oh . . . what?"

Davie felt himself blushing. In fact the questions were of his own invention.

"The first is this—when I met you at the bottom of the Hall stairs, where were you coming from?"

"Where was I coming from?"

"Yes. You seemed to be *en route* from Baxter's Court."

"Well—I was and I wasn't. I'd been in the conference office in First Court—and suddenly Dr. Junge rushed in and said Dr. Brauer had been taken ill. He'd been standing by Geoffrey, so he'd very kindly come for me while Geoffrey pushed on to the dais."

"I see: in at one arch and out of the other in a matter of seconds."

"Yes."

"I was wondering if you'd met anyone or seen anyone going under the archway just ahead of you."

"No. I didn't. Not there at least. I *did* see someone as we came out of the office—but he was coming out of the cloisters and going towards the porter's lodge. A chap in a gray suit. Never seen him before. Is that a useful contribution?"

"Everything's useful. Next question. Can you recollect just who was in the room while you were arranging the screens and flowers on Monday afternoon?"

"Adela and myself and Westlake to begin with. Then Dr. Junge helped. Then Miss Marden and Mr. Krasner came in. A little later, when I came back, Colonel Vorloff was there."

"On his own?"

"Yes. Then we went out together."

"And that was everyone?"

"So far as I know. Colonel Vorloff and I left the Hall about half-past two. There would have been half an hour before people started coming to the lecture."

"All the time in the world," said Davie. "The other question was this. You reached the Hall before anyone was really out I think?"

"Bondini was just outside."

"Did you notice who else was near the door?"

"I didn't know most of them. Mr. Krasner was there: and Miss Marden."

"Were they? They weren't there at the beginning of the lecture. At least, they weren't there a minute before the beginning. They could have arrived while I was going up to the gallery."

"I expect they were late. She was saying that morning that she was always late, and would probably be too late for the Day of Judgment."

"H'm," said Davie. "Come to think of it, that might be a very good idea."

"Blasphemous old devil."

"I object to the word 'old,' " said Davie.

And, indeed, as he walked home along St. Nicholas Lane, 'old' was the last thing he was feeling. He was far too excited. He was thinking, "There's not a thing against that man in the gray suit except that he was in First Court at exactly the right moment. But he could have been the chap I missed coming from the Combination Room. He could have been the chap coming from the oriel window."

Mostyn-Humphries was waiting at the bottom of Davie's staircase.

"You again?" said Davie.

"I have an idea I ought to tell you something, sir."

"Well?"

"You know you asked Baggs the time he put that thing up and he said about one o'clock."

"Yes."

"You asked if he'd seen any sign of anyone else having been on the scaffolding, and he said 'No.' But *I* did see someone."

"*You* did?"

"Well, I happened to be going that way about two-fifteen, or a little later, and I saw someone jump off the scaffolding and make off towards the cloisters. Of course I thought it was Baggs. So when you asked I didn't say anything. I thought he'd got the time wrong. But he hadn't—and so the chap I saw must have been somebody else."

"I see. Did you notice what sized man he was?"

"Well—as I say, I thought it was Baggs, and so I didn't think about it."

"Baggs is a small chap."

"Yes."

"And the figure didn't strike you as *not* being Baggs."

"No."

"So it would have been unlikely to have been a taller man."

"I wasn't very close, you know."

"It was a bright night."

"Well—yes—I do think it was a small man."

"H'm—well—thank you, Mostyn-Humphries. You were right to tell me."

So Davie mounted the stairs to his room and rang up Hodges. He was out.

And Mostyn-Humphries crossed Baxter's Court in search of Baggs.

"That's what comes of reading too many detective stories," said Mostyn-Humphries a few minutes later. "Premature softening of the brain and delusions of extravagant ability for solving problems. Be warned in time, dear Baggs, and confine your attention (as I am sure you will) to the pages of Karl Marx and Schopenhauer and Mrs. Sidney Webb. In moments of relaxation we require to be entertained not bewildered."

"Until you came in this *was* a moment of relaxation," said Baggs, "and I'll be obliged if you let me get on with it."

"Get on with what? Let me see—*Jazz Favorites!* Really, Baggs! I fear you are going to be a grave disappointment to your parents. You'd far better play a nice health-giving game of tennis with me."

"O.K.," said Baggs. "Let's do that."

X

The Courtney children were fond of Dr. Davie. He talked to them as if they were his own age. He was funny. And he had a lot of extremely interesting things, such as a collection of snowstorms in glass bubbles, and a ship in a bottle, some Chinese pictures painted on rice paper, and a special constable's truncheon which had been used by Dr. Davie's great-grandfather during the Bristol riots. Dr. Davie's great-grandfather had hit someone on the head with it, and by a most unfortunate accident had killed him. Dr. Davie also provided a lot of unusual things to eat.

The children arrived at half-past four, and Davie immediately noticed that Richard was uneasy, Clarissa almost frightened, and Abel solemn with anxiety. It was not very difficult, Davie thought, to fathom the reason. Old Westlake, the gardener, had told the children on several occasions that he would send for the police, and now a policeman had actually arrived. True, he had not accused them of anything, but it showed that police could come to the Lodge, which Richard had always declared was against the law. This much Davie divined, though he was rather surprised to find them so subdued. He would have expected that they would have been elated by their sudden importance.

But Davie always had something new. Today it was a fan that had belonged to a lady who had had her head cut off in the French Revolution, and by the time this had been inspected, and Richard had discovered what he alleged to be a spot of blood, and Abel had succeeded in shaking the snowstorms so quickly that they were all in operation together, confidence was restored. Even so, Davie waited till after tea to ask them about the man at the exhibition. The three children looked at each other cautiously.

"He was just a man," said Richard.

"What was he like?" said Davie. "Can you describe him?"

"He was dark," said Richard.

"With a black moustache," said Abel.

"Black moustache, eh?"

"Yes," said Abel, and might have said more if Richard had not nailed him with his eye.

"Why did you go out of the room when Miss Ramble had asked you to keep watch for her?"

"Because he was so ugly," said Abel.

"Yes," said Clarissa. "I was frightened."

And that was as much as Davie got out of them. Still it was something. And when they had gone he made a note on his pad that the man was dark and had a moustache; and five minutes later after staring out of the window in deep thought, he went back to his table and added: "Why didn't they mention the moustache before? Are they lying? Shielding someone?"

Then after another pause he wrote, "The person on the scaffolding certainly seems to have been on the small side. Mrs. Tibbs thought he was Wilkins; Mostyn-Humphries thought he was Baggs."

The telephone rang. It was Hodges. Davie told him about the children, about Mostyn-Humphries, and how Catherine had seen the man in the gray suit. "I'd seen him myself earlier—but only in the gloom of G staircase."

"Description?"

"About thirty-five. Common. Flashy. Small."

"Everyone's small in this case," said Hodges. He

took down the few particulars that Davie could give him.

"Not very much to go on, sir."

"You can confirm at the porter's lodge. Jump saw him."

"I will do that, sir."

"I've been doing the talking," said Davie. "You have something you wanted to say to me?"

"I have, indeed, sir. Since I saw you I've had some remarkable news. When the nine o'clock train arrived at Liverpool Street yesterday morning—"

"*Yesterday* morning?"

"Yesterday morning—there was a woman found dead in an empty carriage. She had absolutely nothing on her to identify her except a ticket from Cambridge. We heard of it of course, but there was no report at this end of any non-arrival. It wasn't until last night that a police announcement on the six o'clock news produced an answer. The person who identified the body said it was a Miss Jane Banbury and that she'd been attending a conference in Cambridge."

"Miss Banbury! I'm exceedingly sorry to hear it."

"What can you tell me about her, Dr. Davie?"

"Not much. She dined next to me one evening and we had several conversations. She comes from some university in the North. A very charming woman, I thought. Is there anything in particular you want to know?"

"I want to know everything I can, sir. This morning a police officer picked up a little hypodermic dart which he had found lying under the seat of the railway carriage. The doctor has found a puncture on Miss Banbury's hand. They're waiting results of an autopsy now, but it's pretty certain that she died in the same way as Dr. Brauer. The immediate question is—what conference members were on that train? Do you know, Dr. Davie?"

"No, I don't. But I'm reasonably certain Colonel Vorloff and Signor Bondini were there. As I told you I saw them leaving the Blue Boar in a taxi at train-catching time. Dr. Willow might know. People may have told him whether they were keeping their rooms for Monday night."

"I rang Dr. Willow just now. He was out."

"I'll try to find him," said Davie. "It's a curious thing that that dart was still there. How big was it?"

"An inch and a half."

"When Brauer was shot the dart wasn't found. It must have been difficult to retrieve, but somebody did it. Either the murderer or an accomplice. But here, when it would surely have been entirely easy to collect it, it gets left behind. Why?"

"There is one fair answer," said Hodges. "Suppose it wasn't fired till just before the train arrived. It fell under the seat and the murderer couldn't immediately see it. The train reached Liverpool Street. It was essential to get away with the first stream of passengers. The evidence had to be left behind."

"Yes," said Davie. "I daresay you are right."

"This isn't the way people commit suicide," said Hodges, "there's something all wrong about it."

"There certainly is. And I'll tell you something else wrong about it. Supposing it was the same kind of dart that killed Brauer—"

"Well, sir?"

"You can forget about that blow-pipe. A crude native pipe like that, even a small one, shoots something bigger and clumsier than this dart they've found. I'm a fool not to have thought of that sooner. This dart was fired by a mechanism."

There was a moment's silence, during which In-

spector Hodges was perhaps wondering if the impli-
cation was not that he was a fool too. Then, "Well,
Dr. Davie, if you can't tell me anything more I will
be much obliged if you can find Dr. Willow. I expect
you'll be hearing from me again, sir."

"Any time you want, Inspector."

XI

Willow was clearing up in the conference office.

"I know exactly who was on the train," he said.
"I was on it myself. There were Vorloff, Bondini,
Krasner and Miss Marden. They'd stayed the night
in hotels. And Jones-Herbert. He'd stayed on in college."

"Is that all?"

"Cambridge people of course. There always are on
that train. Parkin—Williamson."

"Hodges will be grateful if you'll ring him at once
and tell him. That's just the information he wants."

"Right," said Willow, and as Davie was closing the
door he called after him, "And one more. I forgot
Caldecott."

"Why in the hand?" Davie said to himself as he
walked back to his rooms. "You don't aim a lethal
weapon at a person's hand. That's the oddest thing
in the whole story."

Thursday

I

Davie decided that Thursday was going to be a day of frustration. He had known that from the moment he dropped his front stud and spent five minutes crawling about his bedroom before he remembered the demoniac behaviour of studs and found this particular offender lurking in the turn-up of his trousers. Then the post hadn't contained letters he unreasonably expected from several people who had not had time to answer him.

And then there had been Mrs. Tibbs. Hodges had called on her on the previous evening. "He wanted to know about Mr. Wilkins on Monday afternoon, sir. 'Well,' I said, 'Mr. Wilkins made a mistake and come in Monday. When he saw what he done he jumped off the scaffolding quick, took his overalls off and ran through the arch into First Court.'"

"Through the arch into First Court, Mrs. Tibbs?"

"Yes, sir."

"Are you sure?"

"I see him with my very eyes, sir."

Davie cast his thoughts back. It had been only yesterday that Mrs. Tibbs had spoken of Wilkins—but then the matter had been of no importance. She had only said that he had hurried away "through the arch." As soon as Davie had realized that the man was not Wilkins he had built up an idea of his running up the Hall stairs. It had even seemed possible that the chap in the gray suit had been the man. But a man escaping through the archway to First

Court was another matter. Going that way there were
only three people who could have seen him. One was
the man in the gray suit and it would have meant
nothing to him. The others were Catherine and Junge
—and they had said they had seen no one but the
man in the gray suit. It was a puzzle.

Davie sat drumming his fingers on the table. It
was no good pressing Mrs. Tibbs. She would only
take umbrage. And then Davie would be unable to
introduce the subject of the Boys Playing Marbles
and the Rockingham Cow. So he just said "Your
sharp eyes have proved very useful, Mrs. Tibbs. I
don't think I could identify Mr. Wilkins from this
distance."

At eleven o'clock Davie attended the coroner's inquest. As Hodges had predicted, it did not take long.
The Master identified the body; and Dr. Moberley
described the manner of Brauer's death. This was
what Davie was eager to know, but owing to a built-
in resistance to medical words it was something he
was not destined to understand. He heard the splendid phrases rolling out of Dr. Moberley's mouth, but
they brought nothing to him because he had already
surrendered to a delighted contemplation of the jury-
men's faces. This was a serious matter and they were
all trying to look serious. It was a complicated matter and they were all trying to look intelligent. This
they mostly aimed to represent by expressions of in-
tense concentration, with the exception of one rather
stout party who sat gazing at the pathologist with his
mouth slightly open and his eyebrows arched as
though he could not believe his ears. "Paralysis of
the sketal muscle, resulting from the blocking of the
nerve impulse at the myoneural junction." This, he
seemed to think, was going a bit far.

Next to him was a small man with a meek face
who appeared to be intensely saddened by the whole

exposition, though whether by its dangerous implications or by his inability to understand what it was
all about, was happily uncertain.

Davie had just transferred his attention from the
meek man to a tall thin man with bony knuckles
and a high shining forehead when "Iso-chondoden-
drine derivatives," said Dr. Moberley with finality.
Whereupon the coroner, who knew a good stopping
place when he heard it, announced an adjournment
of the proceedings for three weeks.

"I meant to understand all that," said Davie on
the way home. "But I seem to have missed everything."

"There's only one thing to understand," said Dr.
Courtney. "Brauer was murdered."

"And 'in our house,' " said Davie almost to himself. He was thinking of Lady Macbeth.

After lunch Davie returned to Brauer's rooms. He
wanted to get a preliminary idea of what his task
as executor would be. He walked round the room
from cabinet to cabinet, looking at all the familiar
pieces. Everything was in admirable order. Then he
sat down at Brauer's table, opened the long drawer,
turned over a few papers. A square inside a circle
inside a square: Born. A square inside a circle inside a square: Pavik. The sad doodles still marked
the blotting pad. Against the far wall was a bookcase. There were box-files on the lower reaches, and
one of them was sticking out an inch as though care-
lessly or hurriedly replaced. Davie, like Pepys, was
fanatical about symmetrical shelves, and irritated by
the look of the thing, he crossed the room to set the
file level. Then, with his hand on it, he changed his
mind and lifted it out. He would have to look at all
these things some time. It was marked "China O—Z."
Davie turned the cardboard leaves over: O, P, Q, R,

S—several letters from Sotheby's—T—wait a moment.
S for Stumpf: what about that business in Brauer's
letter? But there was nothing there, either to Stumpf
or from him. Of course there might never have been
any correspondence. If Stumpf was a faker he might
have been unwilling to commit himself on paper. But
wouldn't there have been a carbon of some letter
from Brauer?

It was only when he was placing the file back on
the shelf that Davie took in the word "China." Stumpf
would have been "Glass."

Farther along the shelf he found it—"Glass O—Z."
Davie lifted it out and bent back the pages. But sec-
tion S was empty. That is, it was empty of letters.
The compartment did contain one object which Davie
removed and put in an envelope which he found on
Brauer's table. That, as he well knew, was what de-
tectives did, and he didn't want to laugh at himself,
but the fact was that it needed an envelope.

"Well, that's an odd thing," said Davie to himself,
pacing about the room, standing from time to time
staring at the cabinets and seeing nothing that was
in them. "Mighty odd."

On the one hand, the club glasses—Mr. Stumpf—
file O—Z, and on the other, file O—Z—a small red
rose petal, and . . . ? Had someone been there since
Brauer died? A rose petal was not like handwriting,
or a fingerprint, or a hair, or a fiber. Brauer always
had roses in his room. He could have dropped it
there himself. But a rose petal, a fresh rose petal,
it did make sense. File O—Z—a rose petal—and, was
it ludicrously suspicious to add—the man in the silver-gray suit with the rose in his buttonhole? But how
could he have got in? And then Davie remembered
how Catherine had seen him walking towards the
porter's lodge. Perhaps he wasn't a candidate for the
person behind the Combination Room screen, nor

for the person outside the oriel window. Suppose he'd
been at the lecture and seen Brauer die, suppose he
badly wanted something in Brauer's room, mightn't
he have taken this open opportunity to slip into the
lodge and pinch the key to Brauer's room? No one
would have seen him. He could have let himself in
at night, and "My Goodness!" said Davie aloud. "I
may have seen him on Monday night. The man I
thought was Cowl." Ought he to tell Hodges? What
was there to say? There wasn't the slightest proof
that anything had been stolen. A rose petal! Hodges
would think he was suffering from Sherlock Holmes
mania. And indeed he supposed he was. No, he
couldn't possibly tell him.

Davie returned to his rooms.

It was all very teasing. It was quite impossible to
read *The Last Will and Testament of Simon Cassidy*
in those circumstances. But he did manage to make
a start on *Magyar Terror,* which he had ordered entirely because of Miss Eggar's denunciation at dinner
on that first night of the conference. But again and
again between mind and page there fell the image
of poor Miss Banbury. The explanation had to be
simple. Who would have wanted to kill her? If no
one wanted to kill her and it wasn't suicide, then it
would have to be accident. And how could you make
an accident out of a situation like that?

Davie closed *Magyar Terror* and tried to concen-
trate. The result was a usual one with him. He concentrated himself into a doze, and when he awoke
it was almost time for dinner, which he was having
at the Lodge. There was just time to change a shirt.

It was while he was fiddling with his tie that
Davie suddenly stood still in front of his glass. But,
of course, he was thinking—why not? It would solve
two problems at once. But the trouble was that, like
the rose petal—man-in-the-gray-suit theory, the propo-

sition was unprovable. . . . For all that, it was in a high state of good spirits that Davie presently crossed Baxter's Court on the way to the Lodge.

"What do you make of all this by now?" asked Dr. Courtney.

"Goodness, Master! It's none of my business. I've helped Hodges as much as I can—but it's his affair not mine."

"Don't pretend you haven't got elaborate theories about the whole business, Davie. How do *you* think it stands at this point?"

"Well—let me see. Zinty made an attempt on Brauer's life. It failed. And then Brauer died by some other hand—whether for the same reason or another I don't know. He appears to have been shot from the oriel window by a poisoned dart. The dart should have been found. It wasn't—which presumably means it was removed by someone. A blow-pipe was stolen two nights before and found near the college. It bore some indication of having been handled by either a woman or a rather small-made man. On the morning after Brauer died Miss Banbury died in the nine o'clock train from Cambridge to Liverpool Street, and probably from the same poison, and in her case the cause of death *was* found. It was a small hypodermic needle. Miss Banbury's death presents a new mystery—but the discovery of the needle throws doubt upon one of the earlier ones. A hypodermic needle of that sort is not projected by a crude blow-pipe. If the same sort of needle was used on Brauer, then that particular blow-pipe was not the thing that fired it. It was I who brought that blow-pipe into the story—and I was wrong. Even a small native pipe shoots a sizable arrow. It must have been seen or found. Brauer was killed by a dart of some kind —but an up-to-date dart, something not much more than an inch long perhaps, and something fired by a mechanism.

"Besides, looking at it the other way round, I come more and more to the conviction that if a man had come intending to murder he'd have had his plan formed and his weapon with him—not waited to find one when he got here. That's absurd."

"He might *not* have meant to do it when he arrived here," said the Master. "It could have been a sudden idea."

"It could have been, Master, and that's why I don't dismiss Miss Ramble's weapon altogether from the story. I do feel that somehow it belongs there, fits in somewhere. Perhaps someone meant to use it— even tried to use it."

"What do you make of the children's story? Richard's very insistent about it."

"I find it merely confusing. This man—very tall, according to Clarissa; awful and dark according to Richard; very ugly with a black moustache according to Abel. There are plenty of tall, dark, ugly men about. Vaguely the description fits lots of men, but precisely it fits no one I can think of connected with the conference. Anyhow it may not have been this man who *did* steal it. They didn't see him do it. Or if he *was* the thief, he still may not have had anything to do with our mystery.

"I'm not giving much thought to that man. Not because he's unimportant, but because—at the moment—he's entirely unsubstantial. Much more interesting is the unresolved question of who was hidden from the audience behind the screens on the Combination Room side of the dais. That person certainly existed and Brauer knew who it was. No one else does."

"Do you suspect nobody then?"

"As a friend of Zinty, I suppose one must suspect Krasner. But he has as good an alibi as anyone else. Catherine and Junge and Miss Marden all saw him in the Hall. Nor is there any evidence connecting him with Miss Banbury's death. Beyond the fact that he was on the train."

"H'm," said the Master. "Is that the whole picture?"

"Not quite. There was a strange man in college on Monday. He called on Brauer before lunch. I met him on the stairs and had a few words with him. Just after Brauer was shot he was seen walking across First Court towards the porter's lodge. One can't help regarding an unknown man as a suspect when he's just in the right sort of place at the right time. And one other thing. The key to Brauer's room was mislaid that night. And there is some evidence that someone entered his rooms. I don't know if the two things are connected. Somehow I feel they ought to be. But it could have been coincidence. There's nothing in the least strange these days about robbing an art collection. Though in this case nothing seems to have been taken."

The Master got out of his chair and crossed the room to the garden window. Not far away his three children (who should have been in bed—it was past eight o'clock) were engaged in a violent argument with Westlake, apparently with reference to a rose bush in the center of one of the garden beds.

"I can't see why Miss Banbury had to die."

"That is the big puzzle," said Davie. "One could suggest some reasons why. She may have been unlucky enough to discover something that had better not have been discovered. But guessing won't get us anywhere. Why was the evidence left behind? And why was she wounded in the hand? Those are the questions that guard the secret. It's just possible that I may have found the answer."

Dr. Courtney looked up expectantly, but Davie did not go on. "And you're keeping your reasoning to yourself, you tiresome old private investigator?"

"You must let me have some pleasures, Master. Besides I may be wrong and I don't want to look a fool. Not just yet."

"When are you off on your holiday?"

"Holiday proper in a week. Ischia. I did tell you?"

"Yes."

"Geoffrey and Catherine are coming too. But before leaving—that's tomorrow week—I'm going to have a few days in London."

"The Gainsborough, I suppose."

"Yes—small, old-fashioned, quiet, same porter for years. Food all right. B.M. round the corner. You know—Bloomsbury, a very special and to me delectable atmosphere."

"Isn't Hodges likely to want you again?"

"Shouldn't think so. There's the Zinty inquest tomorrow, but apart from that he's got all the news I can give—"

"Except your pronouncement about Miss Banbury."

"I'll have to tell him that tomorrow before I get away. I suppose I shall get laughed at, but it would be naughty not to."

LONDON

Friday

I

Davie was catching the twelve-forty. But before leaving Cambridge he had three calls to make.

"*Me*—walking about at two in the morning?" said Cowl. "Certainly not. I was reading."

Davie retreated downstairs, but the prowler in the cloisters had not been Mostyn-Humphries either. Monday had been a working night for him and therefore he had been in bed by eleven. "From anyone else 'therefore' would have been a *non sequitur*," said Davie. "But I follow your meaning."

The inquest took no time. Davie told his story without mentioning the name of Pavik. The court was not assembled to pass a moral judgement, but only to establish the nature of a death. It did so. Dr. Zinty, in the opinion of the jury, had committed suicide.

Five minutes later Davie was sitting with Inspector Hodges. Hodges was precise. He could tell Davie that Miss Banbury had indeed died in the same manner as Dr. Brauer. Davie was imprecise. He told Hodges the thought that had come to him while fiddling with his tie on the previous evening.

"You can't prove that, sir," said Hodges.

"I know I can't. But it's an idea."

Hodges nodded his head.

"It's certainly that, sir, and you could be right. But how anyone could ever prove it I don't see."

"Nor do I," said Davie. "But, if you can't think

of anything else, perhaps it may serve. Anyway—I
thought I ought to tell you."

"Thank you, sir. I'm much obliged for all your
help."

"At any rate you didn't laugh," said Davie. "Well—
goodbye and good luck. I must be off. I am about
to pursue what is dubiously described as a life of
pleasure—indeed, as I have a taxi ticking away outside at this very moment I must pursue it without
delay. Goodbye, Inspector. You know where to find
me if I'm wanted."

II

Davie settled down in the corner of a first-class carriage—back to the engine, a refinement inherited
from the days of his youth, when his mother had
always insisted on that position together with a monstrous foot warmer—as he remembered it, about the
size of a sleeper—which the railway company was
kindly prepared to supply on demand. It was curious
to reflect that nobody under sixty had ever seen this
metal hot-water contraption. Probably in another forty years all knowledge of it would have disappeared.
History was an absurdity, thought Davie as he opened
his bag and took out a book: half the interesting
things were left out.

It was history that engaged him at the moment. He
had hit upon the idea of enquiring what various conference visitors had been writing lately. It was no
good telling him that it was not his business. There
was a multiple mystery to be solved, and there could
be clues easier understood by himself than by any
policeman. Inevitably part of an author's mind is

revealed in his writing. He thought it was worth trying.

Bondini was not translated. Jones-Herbert's *Antibiotics and the Cow* Davie had rejected as unfair to himself and probably to the cow. But he had collected Vorloff's latest book, *Men from the Jungle,* and Krasner's book of three years before, *The Amazon I Knew.* Willow's *Somaliland Revisited* he had read, but he had brought it along: it might be important. He thought Miss Banbury's book, *A Northumbrian Childhood,* was unlikely to be in the same context, but he had included Miss Eggar's *Poisonous Plants* and expected to find it entirely entertaining.

At present he was absorbed in *Magyar Terror* written in 1958 and published anonymously in America. In England it had been published by Godfrey Kennington, an amiable creature to whom not so long ago Davie had attempted to impart some of his classical knowledge. He had included this book partly because it had worked its way into the conversation at dinner on the previous Friday, and partly because it was a book he could not put down. He had read a lot of it in bed on the previous night: he could not have left it behind. It was not written as a wearisome compilation of horrible facts but as a moral indictment, conceived in long perspective. The style reminded him of Jean Genêt. It was startling, humble, repulsive, sincere, by turns. It was a poem of a book. At the beginning the author had drawn a picture of his life as a child and a young man in Hungary. His pretty young mother, his hard-working farmer father, his young sister. It was all apple-blossom. Then came the war and imprisonment, and then, after a brief freedom, an ill-judged return to Hungary, ending in a new imprisonment. It was of this second and more brutal imprisonment that the

book chiefly dealt, but the author had written rather
as the composer of a large musical work writes. The
subject of this third movement was the Budapest
prison, but against it ran the remembered themes
of the first movement, his mother, his father, his sister, the farm in the days when it was all apple-blossom. And again and again these older subjects as-
serted themselves as though prison and injustice now
were not so cruel as the deprivation of things past.

When he came to the fierce days of October and
November the older themes were withheld and for
a time the author wrote excitingly, as in a fourth
movement, of the opening of the prison, the fighting
in the streets, the escape from Buda, the anxious
flight to the Austrian border. It was one man's view
of a human catastrophe: it held Davie enthralled.
And then, as a composer sometimes returns to a motto
theme, so, suddenly, did the author of *Magyar Terror*
return to his first subject. He was free. The barbed
wire was behind him. The guns and the rumble of
tanks were lost on air. His part in the drama was
finished; and from the past came surging back to
meet him the greatest theme of his tragic work, the
theme that was the real purpose of his life.

I am safe, I am across the border. But I will
not sleep until I have set my vows on paper.

I can forget the prison, and the crimes I did not
commit. I will never forget a time before the
war began, my home, the farm, my mother, my
father, my sister. It is not what has happened to
me that breaks my mind. It is what happened
to them.

My home, my mother, my father, I cannot avenge.
I do not know the hands that destroyed them.

The hands, the two hands that destroyed my sister, I do know. I will destroy them. If I wait till the end of my life.

On November 2 I crossed the frontier with many others. We were kindly received by the Austrians.

Davie finished *Magyar Terror* five minutes before the train eased itself into Liverpool Street station. He was still thinking about it when his taxi drew up at the Gainsborough Hotel.

"Well, Dr. Davie, you *are* a stranger!" said Miss Mercer of Reception, as she had said, with exactly the same inflection, for the last fifteen years.

"I was only saying last week that we hadn't seen you for some time, sir," said Frank, the aged hall porter. "Mark my words, I said, Dr. Davie will be coming soon, I said."

Jack, the lift boy, whose endearing grin was a principal attraction of the establishment, said nothing. Words were not expected. The grin was all. He took Davie up in the lift and came down again half a crown heavier.

Davie unpacked and arranged his books on the bedside table. The next one he meant to read was *The Amazon I Knew*. Krasner had not been a communicative member of the symposium. Perhaps in his book he would explain himself a little better.

Before going downstairs Davie picked up his telephone and asked for the Kennington Press.

"Godfrey—is that you?"

"Yes—who's that?"

"Davie—St. Nicholas's College—Remember?"

"Dr. Davie!"

"The very same."

"Goodness! How are you?"

"In a considerable decline, Godfrey. You feeling terrible too? Good. Now listen—I want to ask a service of you."

"Go ahead."

"*Magyar Terror.*"

"Yes."

"It's anonymous."

"It is."

"Well—I want to know who wrote it."

"Now that I'm quite sure I ought not to tell you— if I knew. But I don't. You see it was published in America. I didn't make the arrangement."

"But you could find out?"

"Perhaps. It depends on how much of a secret the author made of it."

"Well—have a try, will you."

"I will."

"It's quite urgent."

"I'll write at once. Where are you?"

"At the moment at the Gainsborough, but early next week I'm off to Ischia—address c/o Mario's Bar, Forio."

"I'll see what I can do."

Then Davie walked downstairs, ordered tea to be served in the unexpected little garden at the back, and settled himself in a comfortable wicker chair on a minute lawn surrounded on three sides by petunias and roses. Blocked from western skies by the blackened backs of eighteenth-century houses in the neighbouring street, the garden of the Gainsborough Hotel felt infinitely remote. Davie had a ten-minute doze in the sun, and then Jack arrived with the tea, a dish of sandwiches, and a small plate supporting three little cakes in paper cases, one with currants, one with pink sugar on the top, and one confined in chocolate and crowned with half a walnut. Tea at the Gainsborough was ever thus.

III

The Gainsborough Hotel stands in a quiet road off Great Russell Street, its back towards the Museum, its face to a street of pleasant Regency houses, once occupied by the rich and rising middle classes and now by small tidy hotels, and publishers. It pleased Dr. Davie very much, he was glad to be back, and he was prepared to enjoy himself.

On this first night he proposed to take a stroll, and so, after dining at the Gainsborough, he set off at eight o'clock to walk to Shaftesbury Avenue, a task accomplished in twenty minutes by avoiding with commendable discipline all the strange little windows of books in Great Russell Street and Museum Street. He would enjoy them on the way home, or tomorrow.

Having welcomed the whelk stall in Cambridge Circus (perhaps the most nineteenth-century sight in the West End of London) he walked on down the avenue, pausing to examine the drums, guitars, and saxophones, and the windows of the kinky clothes shops: the pink shirts, the floral ties, and the increasing brevity of briefs. Davie wore briefs with the best of them, but he had a hideous memory of having worn long woolly pants when he was an undergraduate: which was absurd.

Thus reflecting on the vagaries of Fashion, he moved on towards the Circus. There were, indeed, disturbing changes. The Trocadero had given place to a "grillette" (was nothing sacred?), a bowling alley and a club; and down Coventry Street the gymnastic Swiss Roll had ceased to roll itself up every half-minute on top of Lyons Corner House. But in the Circus itself the Guinness clock still presided, and the wax lady at the bottom of Shaftesbury Avenue was still graciously employed with her invisible mending as she had been for the last fifty years. Time was when she had actually performed her task in a series of jerky mechanical movements, and had attracted so much attention outside her window that she had had to be restrained at the request of the police. Davie liked her as she was now, silently bending over her work. It was not inappropriate, he thought, that she should perform her invisible mending invisibly.

Not everything, then, was lost.

Davie retraced his steps, turned left into Wardour Street and right into Old Compton Street. Here were the windows that pleased him most: the coffee and the coffee pots; the wine and the pastry; macaroni in stacks, cheeses like wheels, salami like truncheons; and all the shining impedimenta of the kitchen.

Dean Street, Frith Street, Greek Street. He chose Greek Street, and noted with surprise the increased number of doorways where bored young men were inviting passersby to visit strip-tease exhibitions; and the number of other doorways where the most unprepossessing women in London were just not breaking the law against standing on the street. Interspaced with these scenes scarcely removed from the world of Hogarth were the admirable restaurants he had visited so often. It was familiar territory, but grown a little strange; and Davie walked along it more quickly than he had intended.

The beautiful old house on the right at the end of the street marked a boundary (it is the house with the plane tree in the garden, where Sydney Carton used to visit Dr. Manette). Now Restaurant Land and its buzz of light and noise was all behind him; in front, the quiet square.

The gates to the garden were closed, but he stood a minute peering through the railings at the flowers and the strange little octagonal house in the center. The great plane trees spread over all. Much spoiled by the weather, his face made more sardonic than the sculptor intended by the black shadows of London dirt, Charles II, by Caius Gabriel Kibber, kept vigil. Unsuitably he had been sited with his face towards boring Oxford Street, his back to all the striptease, and the twilight Roses in the doorways.

Davie turned right at the church, went down the little street to Charing Cross Road, and crossed over to New Oxford Street. Then, by way of Coptic Street, he was soon passing the classic bulk of the Museum. Sinister in the silence gleamed the window of the Joke Shop. A horrible hairy hand with claws, an appalling sallow face with blood dripping down its chin, a dish of Vampire's fangs. Davie padded on towards the Gainsborough, humming an aria which some days he couldn't remember at all, and some days he couldn't forget. Tonight it was with him and he had just brought it to a surprising conclusion when he noticed he was passing Darnay Street, the last on the right before his own turning to the Gainsborough. There was a bookshop in Darnay Street which he had peered at on previous visits to the Gainsborough. He had never found anything there that interested him. There was not likely to be anything in it that interested him now. But he turned down the street nevertheless, and as he did so became aware of a small board that stuck out at right angles from the house. In gold characters on a black ground he read the legend "Stumpf Antiquarian Bookseller."

IV

Ten minutes later, after a little routine badinage with Miss Mercer, Davie was in his room, contemplating a glass of whisky and a plate of biscuits which Jack had collected for him, and thinking about Stumpf and his club glasses, and whether his story had anything to do with the Brauer tragedy. Brauer's letter had given him no particular instructions, and if there had ever been any evidence of Brauer's dispute in his files it was not there now. Instead of papers Davie had found a rose petal. There was no certain evidence to connect the man in the gray suit with the file; and no evidence at all to connect him with Stumpf. Being where he was at three-forty on Monday, was the man a possible murderer? Or merely a bookseller's traveller who had chosen the worst day in the year for a professional call? The latter one would have thought—if it hadn't been for that rose petal. Somehow Davie couldn't give up his rose petal. In any case what was there to do? Call on Mr. Stumpf and say "I can't find any letters from you to Dr. Brauer. Therefore you must have stolen them"? Of course not. But he knew perfectly well that call on Mr. Stumpf he inevitably would—and probably to-morrow morning, provided Mr. Stumpf conducted business on a Saturday.

Davie dived into bed, punched his pillows into an acceptable shape and stretched out his hand for *The Amazon I Knew*.

There had been five in Krasner's party, all of whom, throughout the book, were referred to by their Christian names—Hans, the photographer, who was a Swede; Jim, the zoologist, an Englishman; Erich, the party's doctor, a Central European; and Tranford, an American, an anthropologist. Krasner did not advertise himself as anything but was clearly a born explorer, and a tactful leader, admirable at dealing with the Indians, though perhaps it was really the gramophone records that secured their friendship. "As the record started to revolve," read Davie, "glittering in the moonlight their dark eyes fearfully sought each other's faces. When the black box began to sing (it was with the voice of Sophie Tucker, I remember) there was a concerted intake of breath from every man around us. They were bewildered, and delighted. So delighted that they obliged us to play deep into the night."

The book was excellently illustrated with pictures of the Amazon, or of the Jivaro, their villages, the wrinkled elders, their bloated hideous wives, naked children spear-fishing, handsome young men fashioning or shooting the blow-gun. Erich had become greatly interested in the blow-gun and arrow poison. One picture showed him watching an incredibly aged man stirring a cauldron. He was stewing the juice of large ants which is mixed with the curare to strengthen it. Davie remembered that Krasner had mentioned the ants at Mrs. Courtney's garden party. The caption said "Erich Learning How to Make Ant Poison." Davie regretted that it was the cauldron and the old man that mainly occupied the picture. Erich stood back to the camera. He was a neat small man in a bush shirt and shorts. One couldn't say more. "By using his singular charm on old Mati," wrote Krasner, "Erich was able to become an authority on these matters. He made exact notes, and, more important for his researches, he eventually obtained some samples of the finished brew."

By the time he put his light out two hours later Davie felt he knew a good deal about the Amazon, but it was about Erich that he was thinking as he fell asleep. Zinty and Krasner. Krasner and Erich. Erich and an ancient warlock stirring a cauldron. Anyone could create a splendid chain of unproved evidence from that. Erich had only to supply Krasner with the poison. Krasner had only to use it. Unfortunately the theory ended disastrously with Krasner and a sound alibi in the Hall of St. Nicholas's College. Krasner had said he had a plan. But if he had he plainly hadn't used it.

The Amazon, they say, has no corpses. If there are tragedies in those waters, the disgusting piranha devour the evidence in a few minutes. Davie felt *The Amazon I Knew* had been equally successful in suppressing its secrets—if it had any secerts. But there had been nothing mysterious about the Krasner expedition. It should be perfectly easy to find out who Jim and Hans and Erich and Tranford were.

But Davie wanted to know now.

Saturday

I

It was another hot day. Davie had breakfast by an open window, looking over the garden to the dark back of the next street. The house immediately opposite looked peculiarly bleak with dirty close-shut windows. Doubtless the never-to-be-seen upstairs of some quite attractive downstairs, thought Davie.

At ten o'clock he was ready to go out. He was wearing a biscuit-coloured tropical suit and he had not scrupled to help himself to a small rosebud from the garden.

"You do look spruce, Dr. Davie," said Miss Mercer.

"When in London, Miss Mercer, I always dress to kill."

Miss Mercer replied with a silvery peal of gracious laughter.

"Dr. Davie will have his little joke," said old Frank; but Davie was already pondering the singular inappropriateness of his words. And not only inappropriate. It was a silly boring cliché. He was cross with himself.

There were not many people about at that time of day on a Saturday. Davie walked down the road to Great Russell Street, and turned left. He knew from Hodges that Krasner and Miss Marden had both been asked to stay in London, pending the conclusion of enquiries about Miss Banbury. He was going to call on them at the Ambrose Hotel.

Yana Marden was sitting in the drawing room reading the *Daily Telegraph*. Davie could see on her face the mark of the last two days. She looked very tired. She looked older. It was not till he had come to a stand immediately opposite her that she saw him.

"For Heaven's sake! Mr. Davie!"

"Good morning, Miss Marden. Don't get up! Let me sit down. This isn't a coincidence. I'm staying near-by and I thought I'd call."

"I'm so glad you did. I don't have to tell you, Dr. Davie, we've been having the hell of a time. Jan has spent hours at the police station. I've been interviewed three times, and on top of all that there's the press. Always a cameraman outside the hotel. One can't go out."

"It must be horrible."

"It certainly is."

"Don't let it wear you down. The police are jolly careful. They don't make arrests without proof. If Mr. Krasner's own mind is clear you can be quite sure that nothing can happen to him. They've got to investigate everything."

"I know."

The glass door winked in the sunlight and Krasner came in.

"Jan—look who's paying us a call."

"Dr. Davie—what brings you here?"

"He's staying round the corner somewhere."

"And I thought I'd like to find out how things were with you. I'm afraid it's all been terribly unpleasant."

Krasner shrugged his shoulders, made a face, and sat down. The difficulty was to go on. Davie had not come to discuss the Zinty case, or the Banbury case.

"What d'you think I've been reading these last days?" he said.

"Tell us," Miss Marden.

"Your book."

"My book?"

"Yes—the Amazon book. I've wanted to tell you how much it has interested me."

Krasner smiled, and Yana Marden smiled too. It was a relief to talk about something different from the eternal subject.

"I wondered about one thing," said Davie.

"What's that?"

"Why were you so anonymous about everyone— Tranford, Hans, Jim, Erich?"

Krasner smacked his hand on his knee.

"I've been asked that before. It was a stunt, and a mistake. One of those familiarities that don't come off. It was arch. It was journalese. D'you want to know who they were?"

"Yes."

"Hans Grieg, Tranford Cornwall, Jim Craddock, and—surely you know who Erich was?"

"No."

"Erich Junge."

"What, Dr. Junge who was at Cambridge?"

"Yes."

"No, I didn't know. What happened to them all?"

"Jim went on some other South American jaunt. Hans went home. Tranford went home—he's got a university job in the States. And Erich got a job at Munich."

Davie felt rather flat. He had not expected to come back to anyone so simple and familiar as Dr. Junge; and he could not think of anything more to say.

Miss Marden asked if Davie was in London for long.

"Only a day or two. I'm *en route* for Ischia."

"Ischia—eh?" said Krasner.

"Why—for heaven's sake!" said Miss Marden. "You'll probably run into Erich Junge. He said he was going there. He's mad on swimming."

The conversation dropped and Davie realized how

artificial the last exchanges had been. There was really only one thing that Krasner wanted to ask. It was not possible to keep off the subject.

"Dr. Davie—is there anything you can tell me about poor Zinty? He was a great friend—and I know nothing, except from the papers, and except what I've gathered from the cops."

"I know as much as anyone," said Davie. "You see, he was talking to me for an hour, immediately before he shot himself."

Miss Marden made a fluttering gesture with her hand.

"But I'm not sure how much I ought to say. He'd had too great a strain to bear, poor man. He thought he was responsible for Brauer's death—and that's the short of it."

"And was he?" asked Miss Marden.

"No."

"Thank God for that."

"I suppose," said Krasner, "the police are satisfied that he committed suicide. I mean they don't think he could have been shot by somebody else?"

"I'm quite sure the police did consider that possibility, Mr. Krasner. But the jury settled for suicide."

"You're not saying what the police really believed."

"I assure you I don't know what they believed. They've asked me a lot of questions—"

"I bet."

"But I'm not in their inner councils."

"What do you think yourself?"

"I think it was suicide."

"Poor Zinty," said Miss Marden in a whisper.

No one spoke for a small space. Then, "Do you mind if I ask you a question about Monday afternoon?" asked Davie.

"Fire ahead," said Krasner.

"I only reached the Hall just before the lecture

began. I didn't see you at the back. But I know you were there immediately after the Master had announced Brauer's death. Mrs. Willow saw you. You were late, I take it?"

"Yes, I was."

"At what point did you arrive? I'm sorry to be nosy. But I'm trying to see where everybody was at that time."

"Aren't the police doing that?" asked Miss Marden. Davie said, "I expect they are, Miss Marden. This is an independent question. Mr. Krasner doesn't have to answer it."

"I can answer it for him. I'm rather famous for being late, and we would have been late anyhow—but just as we'd nearly reached the Hall, I remembered I'd left my bag on a seat in the Close and Mr. Krasner went back for it."

"I see—but at what point in the proceedings did Mr. Krasner arrive? That's what I'm interested in—a fixed point in time."

"I can't tell exactly," said Krasner. "The whole place was in a sort of quiet confusion."

"I guess it was about two and a half minutes after Dr. Brauer had fallen," said Miss Marden.

"You didn't see anyone on your way—on the stairs, or in Baxter's Court?"

"I didn't come through Baxter's Court. We'd been in that wilderness outside First Court. So I came across that court and then through the cloister arch."

"And you didn't see anyone?"

"No."

"Thank you. I'm sorry to be so inquisitive."

"That's O.K."

"Lord!" said Davie. "It's eleven o'clock. I must be away."

Miss Marden put out her hand.

"I hope all's well for you," said Davie.

Krasner made a grimace and pointed a thumb at the windows.

"I won't see you to the door, if you don't mind."

"You mustn't, of course."

At the glass door Davie turned his head. Miss Marden was holding Krasner's hand. They were not looking at Davie. Each was looking the other straight in the face.

"I'm glad they can do that," said Davie to himself.

But the fact remained that Krasner's alibi had a two-and-a-half minute hole in it.

II

From the Ambrose Hotel to Darnay Street was only a five-minute walk. Stumpf Antiquarian Bookseller was open. Davie opened the door and entered a small shop, not ill-furnished. On the back of the door an ancient bell emitted a toneless clatter. Nobody answered its summons. On a table in the middle of the room were a few eighteenth-century volumes. On shelves around the walls were hundreds of books in more modern bindings. Davie spent a few minutes scanning their backs. There seemed to be a large number of works with such titles as *Eroticism in Ancient Egypt, A History of Phallic Worship,* and *The Birchiad*—which proved on inspection to be a panegyric upon corporal punishment in schools, written in rhymed couplets by the Reverend James Parsifloe D.D. (1807). At the back of the room was a sort of office cut off by a glass door. Davie peered inside. In a tray on a counter were a number of packets of postcards, each with one card exposed to indicate the nature of the contents. Davie could not see very well, but he saw enough to be surprised, and was a little embarrassed to be in the act of thus peering when a voice behind him said "Was you looking for anything, sir?" It is difficult to say no you wasn't, when you so plainly were.

The enquirer was a weedy young man with an amiable expression and a mass of untidy hair. In one hand he carried half a pint of milk, in another a paper bag which looked as if it contained doughnuts. He was not the sort of person to embarrass anyone. So Davie smiled at him and said, "I was just looking round till I could ask if I could see Mr. Stumpf."

"Mr. Stumpf?" The young man seemed surprised. "I don't know," he said. "I don't know, I'm sure. He may not be in. And if he is I don't know if he will see you."

The thought of anyone actually wanting to see Mr. Stumpf appeared to astonish the young man.

"Could you try to find him?" asked Davie.

"I could," said the young man but still without moving.

"Then do, like a good chap," said Davie.

"All right," said the young man. "I'll do that. But I don't promise nothing. He don't often see visitors on a Saturday. Not on a Saturday he don't. Matter of fact he don't often see visitors any day."

The young man opened the glass door and deposited his milk bottle and paper bag on the table with the tray of postcards; then, unexpectedly placing his hands together in the attitude of prayer, he proclaimed in a voice of exaggerated piety, "And Gawd grant that Mr. Stumpf is in a amiable mood this morning." After which he very deliberately winked at Davie, turned about, and disappeared through another door on the other side of the office.

Davie heard him delicately ascending the stairs. A rap on a door followed. There was a muffed answer, and then steps across the floor overhead. The young man was soft-spoken and Davie could not hear how his case was presented to Mr. Stumpf, but the voice of Mr. Stumpf in reply was clear and cross. "Who is he . . . Why didn't you ask his name . . . What's he want . . . I'm busy . . . All right. Show him up. The back room."

Presently Davie heard footsteps coming down the stairs. Then the office door opened and the young man beckoned. Davie opened the glass door.

"My dangerous mission has been successfully completed," said the young man in a hoarse conspiratorial whisper. "You are summoned to the presence. Say nothing. And don't, whatever you do, look at them pictures."

Davie decided he liked the young man.

Once past the door to the staircase Mr. Stumpf's antiquarian bookshop became antiquarian indeed. The stairs were worn and uncarpeted, the ascending sporting prints on the wall were dirty and askew. At the turn of the stairs an elephant's tusk stood on a moth-eaten mount. Someone long ago had hung a bowler hat on the end, and it was gray with dust. In spite of the heavy July heat the whole place smelled damp.

At the top of the stairs a small landing divided two doors, one to the left, one to the right. That to the left plainly communicated with the room over the shop, but it was the door to the right that the young man opened, and opened cautiously; it was clear that the china handle and its metal rod were imperfectly connected to the other side.

He left the door wide and went downstairs.

As well as the books that lined the walls there were piles of books on the floor. At right-angles to the window was a large table with a mass of papers on it. On each side of the table was a chair. Davie sat down on the chair intended for a visitor—the one from which the caller sees everything upside down. There is something inviting about letters that offer themselves in reverse. It was a challenge that Davie always found irresistible, and it was not long before he was deep in deciphering.

The first letter he tried was unfairly difficult—

WISBECH

STATION ROAD

SWALLOW and RUTTUCKS

—but he felt amply rewarded by his efforts. What exquisite names people had!

The next, in comparison, was child's play.

CAMBRIDGE

ST. NICHOLAS'S COLLEGE

It took Davie no more than two seconds to read that, and only five more to observe the significance of the fact that he was looking at a carbon. Carbons are kept by the sender. Why was this one on the table of the recipient? The carbon was the top paper of a small clip. Davie glanced back at the door across the landing, then lightly got up and strolled round to the other side of the table.

At the bottom of the letter was a space where the signature would have been on the original. Underneath that was typed the name Paul Brauer. With his eye on the door Davie put out a daring hand and frisked back the papers. The clip contained three original letters. He caught sight of a signature— Samuel Stumpf. Davie hadn't a doubt in the world that the whole clip ought to have been reposing in a certain file at St. Nicholas's College, Cambridge, under the letter S.

The door across the landing juddered. Davie turned swiftly about and adopted the pose of a man deeply absorbed in the attractions of a bookshelf. It was a pity that he had to be so profoundly engaged by two complete sets of the works of Sir Walter Scott, but he hoped he might be carrying it off. As Mr. Stumpf entered the room Davie faced about with a polite smile. He received none in return. Mr. Stumpf was pot-bellied and podgy, sallow-cheeked and shifty-eyed, plainly on his guard and indisposed to oblige anybody.

Davie had a sudden and appalling feeling that he didn't know what to say to him.

"You wanted to see me?" said Mr. Stumpf with a baleful glare. "I'm a very busy man."

"I'm sure you are. It's very good of you to let me call."

"I'll give you a minute. What is it you want?" He pointed to the visitor's chair, and himself sat down at the other. As he did so his eyes fell on the clip of Brauer's papers. His eyebrows contracted in a gesture of annoyance. Then he picked them up, opened a drawer in the table, dropped them in, and closed it.

"Now," he said. "What do you want?"

"My name is Conway," lied Davie. "I wondered if you'd have anything of interest to me."

"Depends what you mean," said Mr. Stumpf. "We have a good many books of interest. At various prices."

Mr. Stumpf actually smiled. Davie averted his eyes.

"It wasn't books at all," he said hastily.

"Just pictures? The expensive ones are very expensive. I can tell you that. We've got some of the

Rowlandsons. If it's only the ordinary run you want you could have seen them downstairs without bothering me."

"It wasn't pictures either, Mr. Stumpf. You don't understand or perhaps I haven't explained."

"Seems not."

"I'm interested in *objets d'art*."

"*Objets d'art*?" said Mr. Stumpf, looking at Davie very hard.

"Yes."

"*Objets d'art*? We don't do that kind of thing. This is a bookshop. As you might see."

"I'm sorry. I must have been misinformed."

"Who by?"

Mr. Stumpf shot the question across the table and it took Davie by surprise.

"Er—by a gentleman I met last summer at Cheltenham—at a. conference—I've forgotten his name. He was a connoisseur of glass and china. He told me to come to you. I'm sure he did."

"He told you wrong."

"Then I'm sorry I've disturbed you," said Davie, rising.

Mr. Stumpf said nothing, but he was looking at Davie with unfriendly eyes.

"That's a pretty outlook, you have," said Davie with a false gaiety which he feared would deceive nobody. "London has so many hidden gardens."

"It's the garden of the Gainsborough Hotel," said Mr. Stumpf. "It backs on our yard."

"Nice to look at if you live here."

"There's no room in this house for anyone to live, I assure you. Books, books, books, from cellar to attic."

"Well—good morning," said Davie, retreating through the open door to the landing. "I'm sorry to have taken up your time. I can see myself down."

It was an unnecessary remark. Mr. Stumpf had not

the slightest intention of seeing his visitor down. He crossed the landing behind him and banged the door.

In the small office the weedy young man was on guard by the tray of photographs and a respectable-looking middle-aged man was endeavouring to pretend that he was only standing there by accident. Unfortunately the young man would not take a hint.

"No, we haven't had anything new in for some time," he said. "Pity really."

"Good morning," said Davie, on his way through.

"Morning," said the young man. "Did you get what you wanted?"

"Unfortunately no."

"Thought you wouldn't."

Outside Davie paused in the dazzling sunlight, watching a military pigeon strutting in the road tirelessly engaged on the quest for provender. He was not aware that he, in his turn, was being inspected by Mr. Stumpf from the window above the shop.

In view of what happened later it was a good thing that Davie turned left into Great Russell Street. At least he had not given Mr. Stumpf the impression that he was staying at the Gainsborough Hotel. He was in fact bound for L'Etoile in Charlotte Street, where he proposed to treat himself to an admirable luncheon.

III

Davie had never thought of himself as courageous. He would have hated to jump into the Thames in a fatuous attempt at life-saving. It is improbable that he would have been much good in a street mêlée. But he had an ice-cold judgement. He never panicked. He had once taken charge of a woman who had had hysterics on a narrow path perched high above an Italian sea. He could do that sort of thing. He feared violence. But he did not fear danger. He rather enjoyed a calculated risk. And it was a calculated risk which occupied his thoughts throughout lunch at L'Etoile.

In itself his visit to Stumpf had been totally useless. Stumpf had given nothing away—unless it were giving something away to be so patently hostile. It was a pure accident that he had seen what he so greatly wanted to see. But now that he knew where Brauer's papers were, how could he not make some attempt to get hold of them? To go to the police would surely be useless. The police (fortunately) require a better sort of sanction than Davie could urge before entering a private house. Davie could hardly pay Mr. Stumpf a second visit. He wondered if he could engage someone else to pay a call, some Bertie Wooster, who would help himself to the table drawer while Mr. Stumpf was absent collecting curiosities of literature from his private sanctuary. Unhappily it all sounded a bit too like Act 2 of one of those Aldwych farces that Davie used to enjoy thirty years ago. Besides it would need organizing. He had no Bertie Wooster. And there wasn't time to look for one. On a Saturday afternoon the Brauer papers might still be lying in Mr. Stumpf's drawer. They would not necessarily be there on Monday.

It was with these thoughts in his mind that Davie emerged from L'Etoile. On the pavement he hesitated, then turned right. He thought it might be just as well to go home the other way, passing behind the Museum instead of in front of it, along Great Russell Street.

Back at the Gainsborough he stood in the dining room, gazing across the garden at the blackened back

of Mr. Stumpf's Temple of the Muses. In every room
except that on the first floor where Davie had had his
interview, untidy piles of books reached half-way up
the grimy windows. All the windows were closed. No
doubt they could be opened in two minutes by an ex-
perienced burglar. But Davie was not even an ap-
prentice burglar, and he rightly supposed that the as-
cent of a water-pipe was beyond his meager agility.

He opened the French window and strolled into
the garden, and then for several minutes dawdled
round the beds, carefully inspecting the roses one by
one. When he felt that he had established himself
as a dedicated gardener he stepped daintily behind
the end bed, with the apparent intention of examining the hollyhocks. Screened from the hotel, Davie
peeped over the wall.

The area on the other side was half the size of
the Gainsborough garden, and utterly neglected. One
or two flowers that had seeded themselves struggled
thinly against the yellow matted grasses. A forest of
willow herb blocked one corner. A tired-looking ram-
bler rose decorated one wall. A cinder path led down
to a back door. Beside the back door was a small
window, probably belonging to a lavatory or a scul-
lery. It was a quarter-way open.

Davie emerged from the hollyhocks and made his
way slowly back across the lawn. He had made up
his mind. He now proposed to spend the afternoon
resting and reading.

IV

Davie knew Willow's book well. He only wanted
to remind himself about the making of the poison.
"The pigeon, with a bewildered look in its sharp

eye, fell over instantly," he read. The Somaliland stuff was most dangerous when fresh, but it could be preserved for a considerable time. That would be essential, thought Davie, referring in his mind equally to the lonely hunter and to the speculative murderer. The poison that killed Brauer must have been brought from a distance, and presumably it was brought for the purpose. Krasner, Vorloff and Willow had written about these poisons in their books— and that made one think about them: but anyone at that conference could have had similar knowledge, and kept it to himself. It was the declared business of all of them to investigate the lives of remote peoples. Even Miss Banbury had been to Central Africa. Miss Eggar had been on a botanical expedition to Central Asia and God knows what unholy recipes she might have collected there.

Davie put down *Somaliland Revisited* and picked up *Men of the Jungle*. Vorloff did not write like a professional investigator. He wrote like a holiday-maker, he was an explorer for love, and he wrote about the things that delighted him—jungle plants, majestic mountains, magnificent men. And animals— especially baby animals. There was an enchanting picture of him bottle-feeding an extremely small bear. In spite of its title, *Men of the Jungle* was a naturalist's book and a history. When he wrote about the arrow poisons of Malaysia and Borneo he did not write as a toxicologist. What he enjoyed was the legend of the Upas tree, and its sociological implications. He preferred to quote the ancient accounts of "the gigantic Poison Tree, whose effluvia poisons the air for miles around," and to speculate on the meaning of that story in a world governed by taboo and priest-craft.

Vorloff had made himself well-liked by the jungle people, though at one point he had nearly lost his

life when he had angrily protested at the brutal
method of killing a tortoise. Grave eyes had been
turned on him. It was not for a visitor to criticize
accepted procedure. If it had not been that he had
cured the headman's little son of a poisoned hand,
Vorloff might have found his grave in that argument.

"I was mad," he wrote. "But then I have always
got mad when I find an animal ill-treated. For a time
I cannot control myself at all."

He had looked pretty mad, thought Davie, that
Saturday afternoon in First Court. But certainly the
fit had not lasted. He had been entirely amicable at
Mrs. Courtney's garden party.

The pages in Vorloff's book about hunting and
arrow poison contained nothing new. As Miss Banbury had remarked, the extraordinary thing was that
these widely separated peoples had all made much
the same experiments and had all arrived at much
the same results.

Davie exchanged *Men of the Jungle* for *Poisonous
Plants*. As he had happily anticipated, this was much
more than a botany book. It was written, one might
almost say, with malice; certainly with zest. Not for
Margaret Eggar the splendid phraseology of Sir James
Hooker. "*Flowers* panicled . . . *Spurs* of upper petals
conical deflexed." In a special case, like "ACONITUM,
L. Monkshood, Wolfsbane," Sir James might add "A
deadly acrid poison." But more often than not he
ignored the baleful aspect of his flora. He made, for
instance, no word of criticism against Deadly Night-
shade. For Miss Eggar "A deadly acrid poison" was
the text, the substance of her book. She did not care
a rap if the upper leaves were "often sessile." For
her the irresistible and delightful question was "are
they lethal?"

"In this modern age," wrote Miss Eggar, "the
poisoner is so ignorant of the world around him that

he has been reduced to abstracting his materials from fly-papers, or ratsbane, or a forged prescription. In earlier times the do-it-yourself poisoner was much better informed. Hemlock, official means of death in classical Greece, grows plentifully in England, hardly recognized for what it is; and who dreads (as he certainly should) the lesser celandine, the buttercup, ragwort, and the wood anemone? A Roman Emperor might die of a dish of mushrooms, composed, and not by accident, of *Amanita phalloides*. The city dweller of the present age is only aware of the mushrooms that are grown in cellars, while that same *Amanita phalloides* (or Stinking Amanita) wastes its fragrance in our English woods. Our Viking forefathers were acquainted with the properties of *Amanita Muscaria*. Today that red-capped toadstool is only known in counterfeit for a gnome to sit upon in a suburban garden."

Attached to many of the entries were historical notes about poisoners and their victims, enlivened by a good number of vituperative adjectives betraying the lie of Miss Eggar's sympathies and her opinion of some of her weaker colleagues. Davie was reminded of a master at school who had always referred to Horace as "that little cad." Such entertaining prejudices did not affect his scholarship; neither did Miss Eggar's scorn disturb her judgments. *Poisonous Plants* was a splendid book. Davie closed his eyes and tried to spell *strychnos toxifera* and *chondodendron tomentosum.* Within a few minutes he was over the boundary.

V

That night Davie went to see an example of the modern theater. As he walked home he was feeling like a man in advance of his times. Was it possible that Jacob Weller, the famous and successful Jacob Weller, should be unaware of Time's revenges, of the passing of fashion, of the fact that use can wear a thought as thin as a coin? In nineteen-what-was-it Society had bubbled with excitement over Mrs. Patrick Campbell and "not bloody likely." Fifty years later a lot of old fuddy-duddies had gone into the witness box and sworn that *Lady Chatterley's Lover* was a work of genius. (Davie thought it a great bore and always had done.) Like a flash all the third-rate writers in the country had viewed the signal and filled their novels and plays with ruderies. And lo! the bird was already on the wing.

A rudery is only a rudery when it has power to shock. "Not bloody likely," in its day, was a thunderstroke. But surely in *this* year of disgrace, the four-letter words, and the four-letter thoughts, were no longer exhilarating. Davie had often wondered how the Restoration wits had been overwhelmed by eighteenth-century sentiment and Victorian prudery. Now he knew. Ten years ago Davie might have been surprised by Jacob Weller's play about sex in a Bayswater boarding house. Tonight he had been bored weary. The fact was that Mr. Weller, the most advanced playwright of the day, was old-fashioned, and who was going to explain it to him? Not of course the critics, who were in one of their famous ruts. Mr. Weller was a genius.

And by the way how did it happen that "the well-made play" had become a term of abuse? In the ill-made play the curtain comes down for no better reason than that it's been up for forty-five minutes. The first man who brings the curtain down on a *coup de théâtre* will be setting the next fashion, he really will be in the van, thought Davie mounting the steps of the Gainsborough Hotel.

Miss Mercer gave him a charming smile.

"I've been out on the tiles again, Miss Mercer," said Davie. And immediately his heart smote him. All these years of facetious remarks especially selected for poor Miss Mercer. Hadn't he worn a bit thin too? Perhaps Miss Mercer would be better pleased not to be treated as an eternal joke? Feeling a little humbled Davie retired to his room. But not to bed.

Sunday

I

Davie waited till half-past twelve. Then he put out the light and drew the curtain. His room was on the first floor overlooking the garden. There was a fire escape outside the window. No lights shone from near windows. The street lights were cut off by the surrounding houses. The sky was leaden. After weeks of fine weather (except for the storm on Monday night) the clouds had gathered in a thick canopy. For Davie's purpose the conditions were perfect.

He opened his window, stepped out onto the iron staircase, and walked softly down into the garden. There were lights behind the dining room curtains. He paused at the foot of the stairs and listened. No one was moving. He crossed the lawn and reached the clump of hollyhocks by the wall.

There was no difficulty in getting over. It was only five feet high, and on the Gainsborough side there was a large flowerpot and an irregular brick halfway up.

Davie dropped softly on the rank grass on the other side. Then he stood still and listened. From beyond the houses he could hear the diminished hum of late traffic. Somewhere to his right a door opened and a woman's voice called "Puss! Puss! Puss! *There* you are, you sly boots. Now come along in and see what I've got for you. Come on. That's a good boy." The door shut. Evidently Puss had determined where his advantage lay. Davie listened again. Then he proceeded cautiously to the back door, keeping to the grass verge beside the cinder path.

It was a stiff wriggle through the window, but he managed it. He flashed his torch and found himself in an ancient and unsavoury lavatory. The cistern was brown with rust. The corners were thick with cobwebs. The waters in the Winchester pedestal were dark and menacing.

Davie groped for the door handle. It turned but the door did not open. It was locked on the far side. In the upper part of the door were two glass panels. The one above the lock was cracked. Davie flashed his torch again and found what he wanted. In the corner were several sheets of old newspaper. He filtered them under the door. Then he wrapped his torch in his handkerchief and pressed it hard against the crack in the glass. Almost without noise a large triangle of glass fell on to the paper below. He put his hand through the door and turned the key.

Two minutes later he stood at the foot of the stairs leading up from the basement of Stumpf Antiquarian Bookseller. Quickly and quietly he mounted to the ground level. A flash of his torch showed him the door to the shop on his right and the next flight of stairs to his left. On the half-landing the bowler hat on the elephant's tusk lured him onwards.

The doors to both the first-floor rooms stood open. He entered the right-hand room, went straight to the table, opened the drawer, and momentarily flashed his torch. The letters were still there.

Davie took them out and pushed them in his pocket.

It was almost exactly at the same moment that a man approaching Mr. Stumpf's shop selected a key, and let himself in.

Davie had reached the head of the stairs on his homeward journey when he heard the footsteps in the shop. Then the inner door of the little office opened and a stream of light fell across the bottom of the stairs. Davie retreated to the back room and stood behind the open door. Then the light in the shop was switched off and the staircase light was switched on.

"There's no room in this house for people to live," Mr. Stumpf had said. "Books, books, books, from cellar to attic." Perhaps he hadn't been telling the truth. Perhaps it was merely an unlucky night and Stumpf was returning for some reason—though that seemed unlikely at one in the morning. Perhaps the feet were the feet of some rival thief. Whosesoever they were the important thing was that they were coming slowly up the stairs. To Davie they sounded less loud than the pounding of his heart.

The steps reached the landing, and through the crack by the hinges Davie saw the visitor brightly illuminated by the dirty naked electric bulb hanging above his head. It was the man in the gray suit and he was still wearing it. To Davie it seemed almost as though he'd been expecting him all along.

"Sam!"

A voice from the floor above answered "Huh! You at last. I'll be down."

For a dreadful moment the man on the landing hesitated. Then he chose the room over the shop and switched on the light.

Clumping footsteps on the stairs announced the approach of Sam Stumpf. He had taken off his coat and collar and was wearing a dirty yellow dressing gown. He looked like an aged and evil tortoise. "You've taken your time, I must say," he called from the landing.

"It was wise," said his visitor in a deliberately calm voice. "I suppose you did take the trouble to read about Brauer?"

"Died during lecture."

"Nicely put. Haven't you heard any more?"

"Whatever's in the papers. Why didn't you come back?"

"A very good reason. I couldn't see him before the lecture. So I hadn't got the money. So I had to get it after. See?"

"Well, did you?"

"In my case, Sam. I had to get in at night and take it. I guessed it would be in the file and I knew where the file was. It was easy. I didn't have to bust into anything. Well, when I was getting it, I suddenly saw the letters. He was a bloke who kept the lot. They might have sat there forever—but if Brauer had confided in anyone they'd have had a meaning."

"A dead man can't prosecute."

"A dead man can point the way to something else and then where would you be with all your extra first editions of W. B. Yeats and Ruddy Kipling?"

Mr. Stumpf belched reflectively.

"Yerp. But, as it is?"

"I think it's O.K."

"Why did you have to be so bloody long about it?"

"Seemed sense to me. You see I was seen about there right at the moment Brauer died."

"Clever, I must say."

"Just bad luck. And I'd had worse luck earlier on when a nosy old bastard saw me calling on Brauer before lunch."

"All right. Get on with it. Where did you go?"

"I reckoned it was risky to come back here, so I drove off to Scotland for four nights and sent you the letters. Seemed sense to me."

"Suppose so."

"You're not very hearty with your congratulations. Anything on your mind?"

"In a way. There was a bloke came to see me yesterday inquiring about *objets d'art* if you please."

"Did he, now?"

It was at this point that Davie remembered the papers in his pocket. If he was going to be caught he might at least make some effort to save them. He took off a shoe and stuffed them inside. It was not a maneuver to deceive a policeman. But it might deceive Mr. Stumpf.

Davie missed some of the conversation while he was doing this. When he was back on his feet Mr. Stumpf was saying, "Yerp. That's what I thought too. I sent him about his business. But he didn't come here for nothing, Charlie. I didn't like it."

"What sort?"

"Oldish. About seventy. Gray hair. Bright sort of eyes. Middle height and a bit square. Deep voice."

"Deep voice, eh?"

"What about it?"

"The old bastard who saw me in Cambridge had a deep voice."

"There you are, you see," said Sam Stumpf. "There's never any peace. Never a clear run. Always something waiting in the alley."

"Where d'you put them letters?"

Davie's heart began to pound again.

"In the drawer over the landing."

"I've read 'em a dozen times but I'd like to see them again."

The man called Charlie got up and crossed the landing. He did not put the light on. The light from the landing fell clear across the table. He crossed the room and opened the drawer.

"Where d'you say they were?"

"In the drawer."

"The table drawer?"

"Yes."

"Well, they aren't."

"I put 'em there this morning myself."

"They're not there now."

"What the hell—"

Through the crack by the hinges Davie saw Mr. Stumpf come lumbering across the landing.

"For Gawd's sake! Let *me* look, can't you?"

He ruffled his hand in the drawer.

"It's that bastard," he said suddenly. "He done it somehow. The letters were on the table this morning when he called."

"On the table! You've got sense!"

"They'd only just arrived—"

"Still—"

"Shut up! I put 'em away as soon as I saw them. But he'd been in the room alone with them. He could have seen them."

"If he had, and that was what he wanted, he'd have taken them."

"Not if he'd only seen them just as I was coming in."

"So what? Did he have a chance to get them before he went?"

"No—except—"

"Go on, you old fool. Except what?"

"Well, I let him go downstairs on his own, I went back to my room."

"Shutting the door?"

"Yes."

"God! You're a fool. He could have nipped back. That's what he done of course."

"No of course about it."

"How else could they have gone?"

Stumpf sat down at the table and rummaged in the drawer. "Dammit, they must be somewhere," he said. Charlie sat down opposite him—exactly where Davie had been sitting fifteen hours earlier. The shaft of light from the landing fell full on the fat face of Sam Stumpf. Charlie's face was lost in shadow. The two of them looked like a specially posed still from a gangster film.

"It don't make any kind of sense," said Mr. Stumpf. "They wouldn't interest young Cecil."

"They'd interest Born."

"He ain't in London."

"How d'you know?"

"Sure of it. Anyhow what would Born care so long as he had his whack."

"You're going to let him have it?"

Sam Stumpf stared at Charlie.

"Of course."

"I don't know why 'of course.' He'll hear Brauer died. He won't know I got the money. Not if you don't tell him."

Sam Stumpf took his hands out of the drawer, closed it, and leaned across the table.

"And talking of shares, Charlie, let's see that money," he said.

Charlie had brought his despatch case with him, and now he opened it.

"I've had a lot of extra risk getting this, Sam," he said. "You understand, don't you?"

"Extra risk? What extra risk?" said Mr. Stumpf, suddenly loud and red in the face.

"I'll tell you what extra risk, Sam," said Charlie in his menacing reasonable voice. "Pinching a key. Climbing over a damned spiked railing in the middle of the night. Entering a room. Finding the dough. Putting the key back. Climbing over the ruddy railing again. We didn't bargain on any of that, did we?"

Mr. Stumpf made no reply, but his eyes narrowed and he pressed his flabby lips together.

"All I was supposed to do," continued Charlie, "was to make a friendly call on the professor and collect. If it hadn't been for me doing what I did you and Born wouldn't get a button. I'm not taking any ten percent for that, my old friend. I'm taking twenty-five."

"But Charlie—"

"Now don't let's argue, Sam, or you'll have a fit. I'm taking twenty-five: two-fifty."

Charlie took the notes out of the case and began to count. And simultaneously Davie remembered something vitally important. If he stayed where he was he had one hope in a thousand. But the two men were on the edge of a quarrel and they were sitting down. They were five paces from the door. He was next to it. It was now or not ever.

Suddenly he stepped across the light.

"What the hell—" began Charlie, turning in his chair.

"God dammit!" said Sam Stumpf.

But before either of them had got on their legs Davie had reached the landing and banged the door.

And it worked. The knob and the rod, which the young man had negotiated so tenderly on Saturday morning, came away in Davie's hand. On the other side of the door the other knob fell on the floor. Angry shouts followed him down the stairs. He did not feel in the least agitated. It was perfectly clear that he would be away before they kicked the door down. Not away by the lavatory window and the garden wall, of course. Away by the front door in a respectable and comfortable manner.

For just one moment he paused on the doorstep and took a deep breath. A few spots of rain were falling. It was much cooler, and his shirt was soaking with perspiration. He turned up his collar and stepped briskly into the night.

Five minutes later he was hailing a passing taxi in Oxford Street. He asked to be driven to Scotland Yard.

II

Dear Sir,
It has been suggested to me that, as a keen collector of glass and china, you would perhaps be
interested in acquiring half a dozen Waterford
glasses which have recently come into my possession and which, I think, are of great interest to
connoisseurs. These six glasses were made for six
members of a Lismore dining club. Each is engraved with a fox's mask and the initials of the
individual member. I shall be very willing to
send the glasses to Cambridge by special messenger for your inspection.
Hoping that I may have the pleasure of hearing
from you, I am

Yours faithfully,
Samuel Stumpf

The taxi ride would not be long. Nor were the
letters. Davie was reading them by the light from
the streets, swaying as he rode, but reading them none
the less.

Dear Sir,
I doubt if my interest in your glasses would be
sufficient to justify the trouble of your sending
them to me for inspection. You do not state the
cost, and I am not in a position to pay large
prices, which these glasses may perhaps command.

Yours truly,
Paul Brauer

Dear Dr. Brauer,
I was sorry to receive your letter because I feel that you really ought to give yourself the opportunity of seeing these glasses. It so happens that my representative will be in Cambridge on Wednesday next. Would you be so kind as at least to examine the glasses. I would be glad of your opinion.

Yours faithfully,
Samuel Stumpf

Dear Sir,
If your messenger will call on me next Wednesday at 3 o'clock I will be able to give him a few minutes. But please ask him to be punctual.

Yours truly,
Paul Brauer

Dear Sir,
I have inspected the glasses that you sent me, and I am sorry to say that I do not believe they are genuine. The price you ask—£1,000—would, in my opinion, be a high one even if they were genuine, and naturally I would be unwilling to pay that money if I am uncertain. Will you please ask your messenger to collect the glasses.

Yours truly,
Paul Brauer

"That's queer," Davie commented to himself. "He knew all along they weren't genuine. Why did he keep them?"

Dear Dr. Brauer,
I was distressed to learn that you do not think
the glasses genuine. Such was not the opinion
of Dr. Born, who has also inspected them. Dr.
Born, by the way, was a medical colleague of
yours in a prison camp during the war. I have
no doubt you will remember him. He remembers
you very well.

Davie snapped his fingers together. But of course!
Born—Born—that was one of the names at the heart
of Brauer's sad doodles. He was almost certainly that
third doctor, that last man to know Brauer's secret.
There was not a doubt which way this was tending.
Blackmail.

Davie went on with the letter.

It would be unfortunate if you two old friends
should be in disagreement. I am sending my
messenger to Cambridge as you request, but Dr.
Born and I hope very much that you will re-
consider your decision and your opinion about
the glasses.

                              Yours faithfully,
                              Samuel Stumpf

There was only one more letter and it answered
Davie's question, "Why did he keep them?" It was
dated on the Wednesday of the conference week, five
days before Brauer's death.

Dear Sir,
After my interview with your messenger I have
decided that I will purchase the glasses which
you sent me for my inspection. I understand
that you do not desire a cheque. If your messen-

ger will call on me again next week I will give
him the money in notes. But I shall require a
receipt.

Yours truly,
Paul Brauer

There was of course no receipt in the clip. A rose
petal was all the receipt that Charlie had left behind
him.

III

The man at Scotland Yard regarded Davie with
some amusement.

"What it comes down to, sir, as I understand it, is
that you have broken into the premises of Sam
Stumpf, and committed a burglary."

"Precisely so," said Davie genially. "On the other
hand I hardly think Mr. Stumpf will prefer any
charges against me, and I am giving you three important pieces of information. First, the man Charlie
has stolen £1,000 which rightly belongs to me as
executor of Dr. Brauer's will."

"You did say that the £1,000 was an agreed pay-
ment for some antiques, or alleged antiques."

"I did. But it wasn't paid over. Charlie helped
himself. As executor I do not propose to pay."

"Did you actually see this money when Charlie
was counting it?"

"No. I was behind the door."

"Have you any evidence of your own that this
£1,000 was in fact in Dr. Brauer's rooms?"

"I heard Charlie say that it was."

"Maybe you did. But can you say of your own knowledge that it was there?"

"No. I can't do that."

"Then you're going to have difficulty proving that it was taken. But this isn't really a matter for us, Dr. Davie. You must get in touch with Chief Inspector Hodges."

"These things are more involved than one thinks."

The Inspector smiled.

"They always are, sir."

Davie began again.

"Second—I'm telling you that Stumpf is at the center of some forgery business."

"That may well be so. But we can't act on hearsay. There has to be proof."

"Of course. But aren't the glasses proof?"

"Not exactly. Dr. Brauer agreed to buy them. People can make mistakes, disagree about the provenance of something. Experts are always fighting over pictures, for instance. If there's anything going on, Stumpf must be caught in the act."

"Still, you might be interested in keeping an eye open," said Davie, his ardour a little dampened.

'I expect we will do that, sir."

"If you don't much care for the first two bits of information, you must care for the third. This man Charlie was in the vicinity of St. Nicholas's College Hall at precisely the moment when Dr. Brauer was killed. He was seen by more than one witness, and I know myself that he knew Brauer. He called on him that very Monday morning. He is not so far wanted for murder. But a murderer is being looked for, and he was present. He's got to be brought in. On the face of it you'd think it would be enough to fleece a man £1,000 for dud antiques. But it could be, couldn't it, that you kill a man for the £1,000 that you know he's got ready waiting."

"We shall, of course, do what we can about this, sir, and I'll get in touch with Chief Inspector Hodges immediately, but you can be quite sure that those two kicked that door down not many minutes after you left. Sam Stumpf will stay by his premises, highly indignant and complaining loudly about burglars. Not unreasonably. Charlie, on the other hand, will have done a bunk."

The telephone rang.

"Charlie *has* done a bunk," said the Inspector, and handed Davie a large photograph album. "The thing for you to do now, sir, is to look through this book and see if you can find him there, and while you're doing it I'll get you a cup of coffee."

"I'd rather have tea, if you've got it," said Davie.

For twenty minutes Davie thumbed through the pages. Tough faces, insolent faces, suave, confidential, trustful, weak, repellent, smooth, scowling and smiling. But Charlie was not among them.

"You see, Dr. Davie, it seems easy. But it isn't. We shall try the railway stations and airports for a man of your description. But since we don't know his car he's probably safely retired by now to some unlikely place or other."

"Such as Ball's Pond Road," said Davie, reflectively savouring one of his favourite addresses. "But not if he doesn't want people to think him a murderer. If he runs away he'll be a fool."

"Yes—but if he *isn't* a murderer he wouldn't think of himself as running away. He'd just be sitting out with his £250, his fair commission for a job done for Mr. Stumpf."

"He's committed burglary."

"Yes. But he's unlikely to see that in the same light that you do, Dr. Davie."

IV

Davie rolled over and looked at his watch. Noon. He had not got back to the Gainsborough till three-thirty. Going to bed after midnight always gave him a thick head no matter how long he slept. He felt now like one of those aristocratic men in the advertisements whose morning-after needs are ministered to by a smiling and provident butler. He knew exactly what he was supposed to order, and did so. Five minutes later Jack entered with a long glass of lime juice and ice.

"This, I am told, is supposed to do the trick," said Davie. Jack looked more than usually amused. He had not suspected nocturnal debauchery in Dr. Davie.

"Oh, what a tangled web we weave," Davie muttered, as he sipped the nostrum. That he hadn't originally told Hodges about Stumpf, and that now he would have to, didn't really matter. It was the deeper thought that was worrying him. He had not told Hodges about Pavik. He had not told the man at the Yard about Born. Brauer was being blackmailed. Davie had conceived it as his duty to protect Brauer's name. So far as he could see the blackmailing had nothing to do with the murder. It would be bad luck for him if it turned out to be the nub of the whole matter.

Had Charlie come to Cambridge to collect £1,000, or to commit a murder *and* collect £1,000? There the man was—in the right place at the right time. Davie had had to tell the police, and from their point of view he couldn't help being a prominent, perhaps the number one, candidate. But from Davie's point of view Charlie was in the clear. If one has a nice subject for blackmail surely one doesn't kill him? Besides, would Charlie be likely to use a curare pistol? They had not caught Charlie yet. When they did Davie might have to own up. For the time being he meant to keep quiet.

Davie rubbed the steam off the bathroom looking glass, and started to shave.

Everything really turned on Mrs. Tibbs, he was thinking. At that distance it would have been easy to make a mistake. Besides, two days had gone by before she mentioned the matter. She could have misremembered. She had said that the man ran off through the arch into First Court. Suppose she was wrong. Suppose (as he had originally imagined) the man had run through the other arch, towards the Hall stairs. In that case he could have slipped in at the back of the Hall and hidden in the crowd. But he would have run the narrowest risk of meeting either Davie or Junge as they came down stairs. He had not met either. Or he could have run on towards the cloisters and so into First Court at precisely the place and time that Junge and Catherine had seen Charlie. Charlie was a certain suspect if Mrs. Tibbs was wrong.

But, if Mrs. Tibbs had been right, if the man had gone through the arch into First Court, then plainly the man could not have been Charlie. Charlie couldn't have been coming through two different arches at once.

But, in that conjuncture, what became of the man Mrs. Tibbs had seen running through the arch? Why had Catherine not seen him? Why hadn't Junge?

And now there was Krasner—Krasner who had done precisely what Davie had always imagined the murderer might do. He had got into Hall late—two and a half minutes after Brauer had fallen—quite time enough to have jumped off the scaffolding and run up the Hall stairs. It had always seemed possible that this could be achieved unseen and Krasner had in fact done it. He had met no one on the stairs, and no one had noticed him come in. The story about Miss Marden's bag was thin and unprovable. Krasner was Zinty's friend. Krasner had had some alternate plan. Why shouldn't Krasner be the answer? Because Mrs. Tibbs would not have it so. Her man had run into First Court; but unless he had done that and then reached the Hall stairs by doubling back through the cloister arch, that man couldn't have been Krasner. Besides, the maneuver would have been unnatural and the time insufficient.

There was only one other explanation that Davie could see. If the man had jumped off the scaffolding a bit later than Davie had calculated, then Catherine and Junge might have been already on the Hall stairs. In which case, of course, the chap could have just walked out of college. Charlie wouldn't have taken any notice of him and Jump was not there.

Davie had gone over the sequence a dozen times. He couldn't narrow it down any further. Besides, he had finished shaving. The bath was full. And the looking glass was covered with steam again. Davie drew a face on it, looking to the left. His faces always did look to the left. An analyst, he supposed, would certainly discover some sinister reason for that.

Then, having tested the water with an exploratory toe, he sank deliciously into his bath.

For the next two minutes Davie was concentrated on the art of having a bath. He was back with his thoughts as soon as the deep-water lolling period began. The trouble was that there were two sides to this mystery. Not one murderer but two. Not one side to the Hall dais but two. The figure at the oriel window had absorbed his attention. He had been forgetting about the original problem, the person at the Combination Room door.

He could have been anyone. He could have been the Archimandrite of Thermopylae, who was staying in Trinity for some reason or other. He could have been some nameless crook. Except for one thing: Brauer had seemed to recognize the person.

Who was about and not in the Hall that afternoon? Well . . . Jump had suddenly appeared after Brauer fell: and nobody seemed to have noticed him before; and there was that strangely assorted pair Baggs and Mostyn-Humphries—they had not been at the lecture; and there was Charlie. If he didn't qualify for the man at the oriel window he could have been the man behind the screen. Except that he ought to have got away sooner. All he had to do was to walk out.

Or it could have been Krasner. He could easily have got from the Combination Room to the back of the Hall in two and a half minutes. Certainly of that lot it was Krasner who made the best sense.

Davie hauled himself out of his bath. He was feeling much better.

"If one must chronicle everything, however absurd," he said to himself, "then one must add Catherine. She wasn't at the lecture. She could have been behind the screen and back at the office three minutes later. Which I don't believe. But there it is (as they say) for the record."

He then drew a heart with an arrow through it on the looking glass, hung up his towel, and walked through to his bedroom. It was half-past one. He had powerful views on the subject of lunch.

V

A good many people have met by accident or on purpose in the galleries of museums. Colonel Vorloff met Miss Eggar beside the Great Bed of Ware at the V & A.

"How do you do?" said Miss Eggar. "This is a better place to meet than some. It's rather splendid, isn't it?"

"The Great Bed of Ware," said Colonel Vorloff. "I had heard of this remarkable piece of furniture."

"I have often speculated how it was used," said Miss Eggar. "I mean, who slept where? It seems like a fantastic relic from a forgotten age, but I understand that something of the same habit prevails in Japan. In Tokyo a whole family may sleep in one room, with father, mother, son, daughter, and son-in-law, all sharing one bed. One would hardly have thought that the circumstances would have promoted the pleasantest intimacy. But apparently they do. The birthrate in Japan is colossal."

"The imagination—" began Colonel Vorloff.

"Boggles," said Miss Eggar. "It is an extraordinary thing, but that verb is only governed by one noun. The imagination boggles. Nothing else does."

"I must remember that. It takes years to master the finer points of any language. The imagination boggles. Well it does, doesn't it?" said Colonel Vorloff, looking again, appraisingly, at the Great Bed of Ware.

"I suppose you have been interviewed by the police about the Cambridge affair," said Miss Eggar.

"Yes. They must have a very difficult job tracing all those people, and checking their statements. Several of the visitors must have left the country before they knew there was any question of trouble. Bondini and I stayed in the same Cambridge hotel on Monday night. He, I know, was flying back to Rome on Tuesday. And I rather think Professor Burgenheimer was on his way to Australia."

Miss Eggar glanced along the gallery in a faintly conspiratorial manner. There was no one else there except two young men, who were examining silver-gilt cups and salt cellars in an adjacent case.

"It occurs to me," she said darkly, "that if they are so eagerly trying to interview two hundred people, they can't have any clear reason to suspect anyone at all. What do you think?"

"I agree. They do not know."

"Besides—why does it have to be one of the delegates? Somebody else could have taken advantage of the occasion."

"Exactly."

"I did not like Dr. Brauer. That I confess. But I did like Jane Banbury. How on earth could such a gentle creature be involved in this sordid affair? It's bewildering."

"I only know what has got into the papers," said Colonel Vorloff.

"My presumption," said Miss Eggar, "is that, maybe, Miss Banbury knew too much. She might have seen something she ought not to have seen. You remember she went to Dr. Brauer's help and raised his head against her knee. She might have found out what killed him. If she did it would be a sufficient explanation for her own death."

The two young men had finished with the silver-gilt cups and were now reading the inscription about the Great Bed of Ware. Miss Eggar turned a little aside and lowered her voice.

"I'll tell you something, Colonel Vorloff. Something rather odd. Just before Dr. Brauer fell he looked sharply to his left as though he'd been annoyed by something or somebody standing behind the screens. You might not have noticed that at the back— you were at the back, weren't you?—but in front we couldn't help noticing it. Of course we couldn't see whatever it was he saw—but we followed his eyes and glanced in the same direction. It was a natural reaction. I wonder if it was a reaction we were supposed to make."

Miss Eggar looked at her companion, and Colonel Vorloff looked back at her: but he did not say anything. Miss Eggar went on talking.

"Now suppose for some reason Miss Banbury had been an exception. She might have seen something nobody else saw. Of course, if she did know something, I admit it's odd that she went off to London without saying anything. But she might have seen something without realizing its significance. I think she may have done; and murderers don't take chances."

"No, they don't," said Colonel Vorloff. "By the way there is a tea place downstairs; I think it would be agreeable to visit it."

"A very good idea," said Miss Eggar. "As an Englishwoman I ought to have thought of it first."

So Miss Eggar and Colonel Vorloff went down the stairs, turned right, and traversed the ground-floor gallery, between the statues and the priestly copes, the angels, madonnas and altar-pieces, to the large and hideous tearoom at the end.

The two young men who were standing by the Great Bed of Ware watched them go.

"You heard all that?" said Mostyn-Humphries.

"Most of it," said Baggs.

"Those two were at the conference. Old Davie would have been interested. I wonder—did you get the idea that the man was pumping her?"

"No. She was the battle-axe type. He couldn't stop her. By the time she's done with him that chap will wish he'd never run into her."

"Up to a point, my perceptive and venerable chum, your observation is right," said Mostyn-Humphries. "But how do you know they did run into each other? Perhaps they met by appointment. Museums are famous places for appointments. Everybody knows that the Russian Revolution was planned in detail in the Reading Room of the B.M. And I am given to understand that the Elgin Marbles is a frequent place of assignation for lovers. That's why they're put so high on the walls—to prevent people writing 'Ed and Shirley were here' and drawing pictures of Ed's and Shirley's ambitions."

"If you and that woman could get together for a nice chat," said Baggs, "it would be interesting to see who'd win."

"Criticism from my old and cherished friend!" said Mostyn-Humphries. "I am gravely hurt."

"Good," said Baggs. "That may result in some improvement in the distant future. Come on down."

"One moment while I pop into this convenient little door," said Mostyn-Humphries. "You go on down. On wings of song I'll follow thee."

VI

In a sitting room in Muswell Hill Miss Weston passed the cake to Miss Ramble.

"Made by my own fair hands," she said.

"In that case I must have one teeny piece. But that's *not* a teeny piece, Madge—"

"Half?"

"I mustn't be fussy," said Miss Ramble hastily.

"I'm sure if *you* made it I shall gobble it up. But I really shouldn't."

"I know you'll have another cup of tea," said Miss Weston, "and then you must tell me all about it."

"The facts of the case are," said Miss Ramble, "that I left the exhibition for twenty minutes. It had been a busy afternoon I am glad to say, but in my absence—while Mrs. Courtney and the children were there—there was only one visitor, a man. Actually Mrs. Courtney had absented herself for a few minutes, and the children, feeling afraid for some reason—I'm sure I don't know why, they are the most brazen little creatures normally—had left the man alone in the exhibition. The miscreant very soon departed, taking with him my smallest blow-pipe. At least so one is obliged to conjecture. I discovered the loss only twenty minutes later, and I am sure the case had not been broached before I went out."

"What a remarkable eventuality!" said Miss Weston, who was not to be outclassed by Miss Ramble in the use of language.

"Four days later the pipe was discovered in a corporation sand-bin near St. Nicholas's College. I made the obvious deduction at once. 'You need not look further,' I said, 'for the instrument which killed poor Dr. Brauer.' But they wouldn't listen to me, Madge—and where do they find themselves now?"

Miss Weston had not the slightest idea, but she gave an amused smile as though she had, and lifted both hands in an action intended to convey critical despair.

"Precisely," said Miss Ramble. "They are baffled."

Then she leaned across the tea table and added in a lowered voice. "It is, I think, a little curious that one of my visitors that day had been a man who actually admitted a familiarity with these weapons."

* * *

Dr. and Mrs. Courtney were also staying in London. The Master had spent the day at his club. Mrs. Courtney had been to see an old friend in Hampstead, and was glad to get back to the hotel.

"I'm afraid poor Jean enjoys very poor health," she said, sinking agreeably into a deep armchair.

"Enjoys?" said the Master. "That's usually the mark of the hypochondriac."

Mrs. Courtney looked disappointed. "That is a shallow criticism, Clive, and you ought to know it. The only thing to do with poor health *is* to enjoy it. It would be much worse if you didn't."

Dr. Courtney laughed. "I am rebuked. You would have made a splendid contender in a mediaeval Disputation, Adela."

"Thank you. I should have enjoyed it very much. Any news?"

"If you mean news from the police—no. Nothing."

"All the way home on the bus I was thinking about the lecture."

"We are all going to do that for a long time. What were you thinking, in particular?"

"About some of the people on the dais after Dr. Brauer fell. Why were there so many there and where did they all come from? It would have been interesting to have a film recording of those minutes—to be able to see how everybody got there I mean."

"It would have been more interesting to have a film recording of the outside of the Hall."

"I'm not so sure," said Mrs. Courtney. "We would just have seen someone running away. But in the Hall . . . I think there would have been lots of interesting things to consider. Not only where they came from, but expressions on faces."

"In American banks," said the Master, "they can switch on a film if there's a holdup."

"Exactly. It's all most unsatisfactory. Nobody seems to be getting anywhere."

Dr. Davie would not have agreed. He thought he *was* getting somewhere, and was therefore fully justified in continuing his round of entertainment. He had long wanted to hear the music of one of the Pop groups. And so, a little self-conscious about whether his clothes were in tune with the occasion, he stole out to the Olympic to hear Jack Wrath (né Cecil Stench) and the Seven Deadly Sins.

"And where have you been tonight?" asked Miss Mercer when Davie returned to the Gainsborough three hours later.

"I have been," said Davie, "to a dress rehearsal for the Last Trump. I have witnessed hysterical tears, and listened to the cries of the anguished and forsaken. I have had my hand held by a weaker vessel who desired the support of a strong man. I have—"

"Gracious! Dr. Davie," said Miss Mercer with a smile which had a new warmth and understanding in it. "I know where you have been. You've been to hear Jack Wrath. Isn't he absolutely smashing?"

For the second night running Davie went upstairs feeling that he had been a long time taking the measure of Miss Mercer.

ISCHIA

I

There had been moments when Davie had wondered if he would get away at all. The solving of the Brauer case was no business of his and he had given Hodges all the help he could. It was Charlie who held him up. He and Jump were the only persons who could hope to identify him. It was therefore important that Davie should be at hand when Charlie was eventually detected.

On Monday a holiday-maker at Rhyl was questioned; on Tuesday a bank clerk at Southend. On Wednesday morning a Baptist minister had been cornered in Swansea. But on Wednesday afternoon the real Charlie himself had been seen coming out of a cinema at Dalston. ("There now!" said Davie. "I said he'd go to Ball's Pond Road.") And that same evening Davie had picked him out at an identity parade. On Thursday Charlie spent several hours in "helping the police." On Friday Davie was told that there would be no objection to his starting on his holiday—and so here he was in Forio, agreeably installed in a villa with Catherine and Geoffrey Willow.

The police had not really been amused by the Charlie incident, for the plain fact was that there was nothing against Charlie. He had been in Cambridge because he had an appointment with Brauer. He had been at the back of the Hall and heard the announcement that Brauer was dead, and had left the Hall and the college at once. He was not returning to London and had proceeded by car to Scotland. He had not stayed anywhere that night because he liked night driving. The only thing was that he didn't seem to have got very far. If he'd left Cambridge at five o'clock why hadn't he got farther than Barnard Castle by lunch time next day? It appeared that Charlie had spent the morning viewing York. He had it all pat. Furthermore, as the police had already pointed out, there was nothing but hearsay evidence of Charlie's entering Brauer's rooms and stealing £1,000. Charlie naturally denied it flatly. Davie felt a bit bruised about the whole business. Whatever anyone else thought, he believed that his adventure had been enormously valuable. It had enabled him to identify Charlie, and Charlie's precise position on Monday afternoon was enabling him now to establish a pinpoint in a time-table. Charlie had seen Catherine and Junge. Catherine and Junge had seen him. There was no doubt about that. And none of them had seen anyone else.

Davie had gone over the timetable again and again. It ran like this.

Take X as the time when Brauer fell. Allowing for the confusion, allowing for a few necessary words with Willow, Junge had perhaps left the Hall at X plus three minutes. He would have reached the office at X plus three and a half minutes. At X plus four and a half minutes Junge and Catherine would have been leaving the office.

Charlie left the hall the moment he heard the Master's announcement. If that had been at X plus four minutes, he would have reached the cloister arch into First Court at X plus four and a half minutes. Across the court he saw Catherine and Junge. They saw him.

Davie had waited to hear the Master's announcement. But he had farther to go than Charlie. He would have reached the bottom of the Hall stairs at X plus four and three quarter minutes. There he met Catherine and Junge.

Between the times when Brauer fell and when Junge left the Hall there were three minutes, during which anyone could have entered it. Krasner did enter it half a minute before Junge left; but nobody (except Miss Marden) had noticed the fact.

Between the times when Junge and Charlie left the Hall there was another whole minute—a minute in which the murderer could have run upstairs without meeting anyone. If he had entered the Hall no one would have noticed. There was also a shorter gap between the time when Charlie left the Hall and when Davie came down from the stone gallery. But these opportunities were all confuted by Mrs. Tibbs. Mrs. Tibbs was quite certain that the person had not gone that way. The person had run into First Court.

The possibility that the murderer had been slower than Davie had calculated now seemed to him a very weak explanation. If getting down and changing could have taken as long as four and a half minutes then Catherine and Junge would have missed him. It was the easiest solution, but it was shot down as usual by the contrary voice of Mrs. Tibbs. "He was out of his shed in no time and off through the arch," she had said, and Mrs. Tibbs had been speaking naturally and under no compulsion.

There remained one other possibility which Davie had not spotted earlier. Suppose the getaway had been quick (and that was what Mrs. Tibbs had said), the person might have run past the conference office unnoticed by Catherine, and hidden temporarily on the next staircase, C staircase, the one on which Junge and Vorloff were staying. That would have been accomplished before Charlie was there to see. The only

thing against that one was that it was surely unlikely
that Catherine would have failed to see somebody
running past the window.

Unless . . . there was of course an obvious explanation why Catherine might not have seen anybody.
But it was an explanation that he couldn't bring himself to believe. A professional investigator would not
be governed by his affections and emotions. But Davie
was not a professional and he was governed by them.
He rejected the possible explanation.

So there was something wrong about every possibility and that meant that somewhere, somehow, an
inaccuracy had established itself as truth. It might
not be deliberate, but somewhere in the story there
was a lie. Davie hoped it had not been told by Catherine.

When he reached that point in his reconstruction
Davie would leave wherever he was and stroll down
the main street of Forio. Mario's bar was the ultimate
object.

II

Davie went into a small shop to buy writing paper.
The aged proprietor rose to his feet with a happy
smile. He could speak English. "I have very nice
paper," he said. "Black." And then, reading some
wonder in the darkness of Davie's eyes, he added with
embarrassment, "I mean white."

That was the charm of Forio. The inhabitants had
a long way to travel. There were not many visitors
because there was not much accommodation; and although the citizens were eager to collect all they could,
exploitation was not as yet properly organized, prices
were reasonable, misunderstandings delightful. Hand-

some young men drove juddering motor carrozzos along stony roads, occasionally surprising their customers by stopping to talk to their uncles, or to offer their mothers a lift. Tar impinged upon the beaches. Bougainvillaea dripped from the walls. Oleanders lined the ways. And Mario's bar was reliably entertaining.

Mario's was where you collected your letters. Davie picked up his and sat down outside at a corner table partly shaded by an oleander. Six ignoble-looking communications he set aside. The seventh he opened. "The author of *Magyar Terror* was Erich Kossuth," wrote Godfrey Kennington. "I don't know a thing about him." Of course you don't, dear silly old Kennington, thought Davie. Nor, I daresay, does anyone else. First the book's anonymous. Now it's probably pseudonymous. Oh well . . . it will emerge in time.

On the other side of the small area claimed from the public thoroughfare by Mario sat eight men of assorted ages, all elegantly turned out, remarkably blessed by the sun. They kept up a running fire of light badinage and as they were only a few feet away Davie could hear the whole of it. It made him think of Dr. Johnson's resounding denunciation. "This merriment of parsons is mighty offensive." What, Davie wondered, would the doctor have said of the conversation of these airy gentlemen? It was quick-witted and not unentertaining, but it had a dedicated tendency to revolve round and around the same point. He could imagine Boswell cooking up one of his ponderous questions.

BOSWELL: Is not the conversation of these gentlemen addressed to the Affections, Dr. Johnson?

JOHNSON: Sir, the conversation of Queans is nothing. It is as exhausting as it is inexhaustible.

* * *

But on one of Boswell's off days—the sort of day when he provoked his patron by asking him why a pear had a different shape from an apple—the Doctor might have offered a contrary opinion.

BOSWELL: Is not the conversation of these gentle-men addressed to the Passions, Dr. Johnson?

JOHNSON: Sir, their conversation is not addressed to you. If you are unable to comprehend its drift, they will be very little concerned I assure you.

On the whole Davie thought his neighbours were rather fun. Besides he was a bit of a dandy himself. He admired the sun tans and enjoyed the sartorial elegancies.

Geoffrey and Catherine Willow entered the little enclosure.

"Guess what," said Catherine.

"Shan't," said Davie. "Tell me."

"Guess who," said Willow.

"Who?—that's easier. Dr. Junge."

"Is that second sight, or divine inspiration?" said Catherine.

"Neither. I heard he was going to be here. So I was expecting him."

"He's staying over at Porto d'Ischia but he came here because he likes the beach. He's a mighty swim-mer and goes out miles. We found him simmering on the sand. He's nice."

"Yes. I remember. I liked him."

"We've asked him to lunch," said Willow.

"I'm going in," said Catherine. "See you in half an hour."

"Right."

Geoffrey Willow and Davie sat on with a Campari.

"Funny Junge being here."

"Not so funny as my being here," said Davie. "I don't swim. I've no intention of going up the volcano. I'm only thinking, and I could do that in Ponder's End."

"That I seriously doubt. What are you thinking about?"

"Brauer, of course. I keep going over it in my mind. So much is known, or seems to be. But if Brauer was killed by someone at the oriel window, the person Mrs. Tibbs saw—how did he get away without being seen by anyone else? That's the big question, the large bafflement. Mrs. Tibbs saw him get off the scaffolding and run through the arch into First Court. Yet Catherine didn't see him enter First Court though the conference office was next door to the arch."

"If she were working she wouldn't have been looking out of the window," said Willow. "Might have been looking precisely the other way."

"True; it's odder that Junge didn't see him when he left the Hall. He can only have missed him by seconds, and if he'd missed him on the near side of the arch you'd still have expected that he might have seen him farther off, by the lodge, or in the distance in the Long Walk. But no. The only person Junge and Catherine both saw was the man in the gray suit, and he was geographically in the wrong place, coming out of the cloister arch. Of course if Jump had been where he ought to have been, in the lodge, *he* would have seen something. But you can trust Jump to be unhelpful. On this particular day he had developed an improbable thirst for knowledge and had ambled off to look important at the back of the Hall."

"Was Mrs. Tibbs certain the man went off into First Court?"

"So she said."

"Suppose she made a mistake."

"Unlikely."

"But suppose she did, and the chap went through the other arch towards the Hall stairs."

"My dear Geoffrey, I've gone over that possibility again and again. Suppose that and you can suspect everyone who was near the door."

"That is precisely what I do," said Willow. "To be safely in the Hall, surrounded by people, mostly strangers, at the very moment the murderer was supposed to be escaping—that would be excellent cover and an alibi in one."

"Excellent," said Davie. "I've thought about it a lot. But who can speak for whom? Do *you* know who was on your right?"

"Yes—Bondini."

"Oh—you *can* be sure about that?"

"Yes—I think so. And on my left, at first, Vorloff. He elbowed farther off when the lecture began: and then, a little later, Miss Marden came in."

"No Krasner?"

"I didn't see him."

"He was there a bit later on. Catherine saw him."

"I didn't."

"So—when Brauer fell, Bondini was on one side of you and Miss Marden on the other. Anyone else near the door?"

"Several people I didn't recognize. It was a public do."

"Did you see Jump?"

"Not till later, when he followed me up the Hall."

"H'm—well, you've established the presence of two people at the important moment—but you've lost Vorloff and you haven't found Krasner, and you didn't see Jump, and if one of those people you didn't know had come in late you wouldn't have noticed, or at least wouldn't have remembered."

"No. I wouldn't."

"If the murderer gets into the Hall we've lost him, I think," said Davie.

"If he doesn't he vanishes into thin air and that's worse," said Willow.

"Unless—"

"Unless what?"

Davie didn't answer. He was apparently staring at a beautiful young man in sky-blue jeans at the next table; but (like Mrs. Jellyby in *Bleak House* who spent so much of her time looking into Africa) his eyes were really fixed on the scenes he had witnessed in St. Nicholas's College during the five minutes after Brauer's death. One scene in particular.

"Unless what?"

"I'm sorry. I suddenly thought of something."

"To the point? To this point?"

"I think so," said Davie, staring steadily at Willow. "I think so. I'm not quite sure. Let's go back. It's lunch time."

Willow gathered up the unopened letters on the table. "It would be a pity to leave all your post behind."

"Thanks," said Davie. "But actually it wouldn't have mattered in the least."

"That old sport in the pink shirt," said a middle-aged sport in a lemon one, "was looking very hard in this direction. I *do* hope—"

"It's no good *your* hoping, Rex," said the young man in the sky-blue jeans. "He was looking at *me*."

"That," said Rex, "is an example of one of your many and lamentable fixations."

"As a matter of observation he wasn't looking at either of you," said a third man. "He was finding something in his mind and saying 'Eureka!' like that chap in his bath who suddenly discovered his principle."

"Really! If you're going to be obscene I shall be obliged to stay," said Rex.

And so the conversational wheel went round on its familiar axis.

III

Lunch had been pleasant, though Davie had been rather quiet and abstracted. Afterwards he retired to his room, leaving Willow and Catherine and Junge talking on the terrace. But it was not to indulge in a siesta. He was in a high state of excitement. To his entirely amateur way of thinking the whole entanglement had suddenly untied. A professional investigator might have objected that there was too much guesswork in his theory. Well, what of it? He was not the police. He was only considering the evidence in order to satisfy himself. Never mind how he had got there, the point was that he now felt he knew the answer. The question that immediately concerned him was what he was to do with his knowledge. He certainly wasn't going to create an appalling scandal by talking about it openly; and yet he wanted to expound his theory to someone, to support himself on one critical opinion.

From his window he could hear Junge and the Willows talking on the terrace below. Two men talking, for Catherine was mainly listening. It reminded him of that other conversation he had partly overheard on the first night of the conference, when Zinty had spoken to Krasner about Yana Marden, and gone on to discuss the plot against Brauer.

Presently Catherine got up and said goodbye: she was going to have her lie-down. That was a little help. But even now two people was one too many, and he had decided that it was Junge he wanted to confide in.

Davie went downstairs and out at the back entrance. There was a seat in a sort of oleander grove from which he could watch the path from the villa.

He did not have to wait long. Geoffrey Willow said goodbye at the gate and Junge came down the path alone.

Davie called to him.

"Hullo, Dr. Davie! I thought you were snoozing."

"I couldn't. And there was something I wanted to say to you privately. So—not to make too fine a point of it, I'm here by design. I'm waylaying you."

"Aha! And what do I have to do?"

"I wanted to ask if you'd come down to the beach with me—somewhere where you can bask, and I could tell you something I've got very much on my mind. I've got to tell someone, and I think you're the most suitable person. Can you spare the time?"

"Yes, indeed."

"Thank you. This path leads to the first beach. At this time of day there will be only those insensate holiday-makers who can't bear to lose a moment of it."

"Like us," said Junge.

"It's the Brauer case I want to talk about."

"I've been asked a lot of questions on that subject," said Junge. "But nobody has *told* me anything. If *you* can, I'll be interested."

IV

Junge and Davie had arranged themselves comfortably on the sand in the shadow of a rock.

"I must explain," said Davie, "that in my efforts to sort out this mystery I have made a point of reading, or, in some cases, rereading the books which had been written by various members of the symposium. I thought they might give some lead to a man's character as well as to the details of his life. And so I reread Colonel Vorloff's fascinating books, and particularly his latest, *Men from the Jungle*. I also looked at Miss Eggar's learned and highly entertaining *Poisonous Plants*. And I became deeply interested in a book called *Magyar Terror*, published seven years ago. Do you know it? It's a poem of a book. A terrible poem. I was fascinated by it. It's a great piece of writing, I think. But what held my attention in particular was the last page. Have you read the book?"

"Indeed I have. As a Hungarian I couldn't miss it."

"You are Hungarian? I didn't know that."

"I've a German name. I work in a German university. But I am Hungarian."

"That's very interesting. Well . . . if you've read *Magyar Terror* you'll remember the extraordinary way the author returns to his original theme."

"I do."

"His own loss of life in prison is brushed aside as he remembers again the sufferings of his family."

Davie dived for his pocketbook and took out a piece of paper.

"I've got it here. 'My home, my mother, my father, I cannot avenge. I do not know the hands that destroyed them. The hands, the two hands, that destroyed my sister, I do know. I will destroy them. If I wait till the end of life.

"'On November 2nd I crossed the frontier with many others. We were kindly received by the Austrians.'

"I find it very moving—but to me, who had heard a story something like this from Zinty; to me, who was looking for a man who had waited twenty years to kill a man who had killed his sister, it was—to put it mildly—it was interesting."

Davie paused so long that Junge had to look up to see if there was a reason.

"Zinty had seemed to know something about the book," Davie went on. "I knew that his friend Krasner had been through the Troubles. I wondered if this anonymous book might be by him. So then I read *The Amazon I Knew,* and I realized at once that the author of that book could never have written *Magyar Terror.* The Amazon book is factual. I needn't ask if you've read it. Of course you have. It's partly about you."

"Yes," said Junge.

"It's a report on an expedition, and social scientists will have found it very remarkable, I don't doubt. But for me it's a repulsive book: too many lice, snakes, alligators, piranhas, witch doctors and head-shrinkers. There's a lot in it about hunting, the making of blow-pipes, the brewing of poison."

"And a picture of me watching ants being stewed for the purpose," said Junge.

"You will understand how one's mind plunges along. Krasner was Zinty's friend: no question of that: and he seems to have been close to the sort of poison that killed Zinty's enemy. I found that interesting. One couldn't not notice it."

Again Davie stopped, and again Junge looked up at him as though to ask why. Davie was staring steadily at his fingers.

"I also re-read parts of Willow's book *Somaliland Revisited,*" he went on after a long pause. "D'you know that one?"

"Certainly. On my sort of subject it's an authority."

"You'll remember then that it's the only one that contains an eye-witness account of the whole process of making the poison. Willow himself is such a jolly little man that it always surprises me to read that graphic sinewy prose of his. That bit, for instance, about the acrid smoke, and the stench of the stuff: it almost makes one's eyes smart to read it. Do you remember the headache he was warned against and didn't believe in, but got. All those details. I feel I was there myself."

"I agree. It's an extraordinary book. But Dr. Willow's an extraordinary man."

"Had you ever met him before?"

"Yes—last year. He was at a conference in Philadelphia."

"I remember."

"That was really why Krasner and Zinty came to this conference in Cambridge. He told them about it and asked them to come. We saw quite a lot of him. Zinty especially. He and Willow were rather friendly together. They met later in New York, I think."

"Really?" said Davie. "I hadn't realized you'd all known each other before. Willow never mentioned it."

Twenty-five yards from where they were lying the young man who had been wearing light blue jeans and was now wearing nothing but a light blue triangle, emerged from the sea, and stood against the sun, a figure of mahogany.

"When I was that age," said Davie, "we wore the most ghastly bathing dresses that covered one from knee to shoulder. Plain navy blue usually. Blue and white horizontal stripes were considered a bit dashing. It is a matter for regret."

"Whatever Fashion considers right *is* right," said Junge. "There is no other judgment. What was considered dashing forty years ago I've no doubt *was* dashing."

"It is kind of you to think so," said Davie, "but I never remember feeling as splendid as these young men evidently do."

The young man in the light blue triangle walked

back into the water. As in some seascape by Botticelli the sunlit waves caressed him for a formal minute. Then he dived and streaked off towards the western arm of the bay.

"As I was saying before my attention was diverted by the pursuit of beauty," said Davie, "I found all these books extremely interesting."

"They are. But they don't take you very far, do they? I mean with reference to this mystery."

"No, they don't. I'm only telling you the way I burrowed along. I daresay I'd have come to a dead end if it hadn't been for a conversation I had with Geoffrey Willow this morning, which suddenly and quite accidentally revealed an enormous basic lie which has bedevilled the whole investigation. It also suggested to me for the first time that I had been totally misled from the start by Zinty's friendship with Krasner. I had overheard Zinty on the first evening of the conference talking to Krasner. He was warning him not to be carried away by the charms of Miss Marden. And then he continued talking about some plan. I assumed there were two people in the room. I only heard two voices. I now think there were three—Zinty, Krasner, and another. Only the early remarks were addressed to Krasner. The rest I think were addressed to the third party. The answering voice did not say very much and it wasn't as clear as Zinty's. I assumed it was Krasner's voice. I'm pretty sure now I was wrong."

"Excuse my interrupting," said Dr. Junge, "but may I ask when and where you heard this conversation?"

"I was sitting at my window on M staircase. The voices came from the set below mine—Zinty's. When? It would have been about half an hour before the cocktail party on that first evening of the conference."

"Curiously enough I was in the Dutch Garden at about that time, and I recall seeing Dr. Willow showing Krasner the way to his rooms."

"That's interesting," said Davie. "It's confirmation of Krasner's whereabouts. . . . Well—as I was saying, I now believe there was also someone else in Zinty's room, and I think that Zinty and this other person were engaged in a plot to kill Brauer. I'm not sure how much you know, Dr. Junge—but just before poor Zinty committed suicide he told me his reasons for killing Brauer (as he believed he had done) and he earnestly swore to me that Krasner had no part in the plot. At the time I thought he was protecting Krasner. I now think that he told the truth. Krasner may have been a go-between, but Zinty and the other person were the executioners."

"You will not forget that Krasner is an old friend of mine, Dr. Davie."

"Indeed I know that very well."

"I am sure Krasner would have had no real part in any plot to murder."

"I hope you are right. Indeed I believe so."

Davie paused.

"Am I being logical? That's what I want to know. That's why I've asked you to listen to me."

"Logical—perhaps. It's proven facts that seem to be lacking."

"I'm coming to some of them now."

"Please continue."

"Zinty had a plan—the main plan. We know that. The other man had an alternative. That much I heard them say. From what we know to have happened I presume that the other man was prepared to shoot Brauer if necessary, but was undecided how to manage it. He knew about the scaffolding outside the oriel window; and when he heard on Sunday afternoon about the screens on the dais, he saw his chance.

Then, when he realized that Brauer was still alive on Sunday night, he decided to act—without telling Zinty what he was going to do. So he made the breach in the oriel window that night, and on the Monday he probably saw to it that the screens were well placed. He also made a point of being seen in Hall before the start of the lecture. Then he slipped away, put on Wilkins's overall, climbed the scaffolding, shot Brauer, and then instead of running away, or attempting immediately to mingle with the crowd, you went—"

"*I* went?" said Junge, sitting bolt upright.

"I think so," said Davie; "you went straight to Mrs. Willow, giving her the impression that you had been sent by Dr. Willow. That was the big basic lie. It was cool and extremely clever. She never doubted that you had come from the Hall, and as there was no particular reason to refer to it, no one ever discovered that you hadn't. But someone did see a man leave the scaffolding and run through the arch—my bed-maker: and at the identical time Catherine Willow saw you come running through the arch to look for her. Neither of you saw anyone else. I had found all that extremely mysterious until this morning when I asked Geoffrey Willow to name the people near him at the lecture. There was Miss Marden and Bondini, and a reference to Vorloff, and several unrecognized persons —but you, the person he was supposed to have despatched to Catherine he never mentioned. He didn't mention you because you weren't there. At that moment you were just jumping off the scaffolding. No one saw anyone escaping because nobody *was* escaping. The man who shot Brauer was calmly re-entering the Hall as an aide to one of the conference secretaries. Nor was that all. You must have boldly slept in college that night, or at any rate, stayed long enough to replace the glass."

Dr. Junge lay quite still on the sand, his arms behind his head, his eyes fixed on the horizon.

"That is a very ingenious theory, Dr. Davie," he
said. "What are you going to do about it?"

"Nothing, Dr. Junge."

"Nothing?"

"There are four good reasons for doing nothing.
The first is that there has been enough tragedy. The
characters in *Magyar Terror* are mostly dead. Brauer
is dead. Zinty is dead. Miss Banbury is dead."

"I was sorry about her," said Junge. "I hope you
are not under the delusion that I killed her."

"You didn't want to kill her. Let's leave it at that."

"Go on," said Junge.

"Secondly, if the story that Zinty told me is true,
I'm bound to tell you that I don't blame either of
you. Don't think I'm in favour of the ordinary man
taking the law into his hands: but if murder can be
justified I suppose this one was. If Brauer had been
tried by a court he'd have been condemned."

"To a few years' imprisonment," said Junge.

"Thirdly, you'll be surprised to know that I was
fond of Brauer, and, in spite of all I now know, I still
am. I think he didn't want to do things that he was
bound to do. There were some splendid characters
who refused. He wasn't one of them. But he lived on
to be another man. I don't want to see his name
blackened. If anyone favours another, believing him
to be virtuous, and is deceived—"

"Yet it is honourable to have been deceived. Plato,
I think."

"Plato. There was much good in Brauer. I don't
forget it."

"And fourthly?"

"Fourthly, my dear man, although I'm sure that
what I've told you is true, and although you've made

no attempt to deny it, what sort of a hash do you think a defense counsel would make of my argument? The police haven't got the poison gun. There were no fingerprints on the glass. The rain wiped out any footprints on the scaffolding. There wasn't a thing inside the workman's hut. I haven't proved that you shot Brauer. I've only deduced it. I needed to tell you all this. But I don't mean to tell anybody else."

"Suppose somebody else comes to the same conclusions?"

"I don't think they will. You didn't tell Mrs. Willow that her husband had sent you?"

"No."

"She presumed it. Well—she presumed wrong."

Junge rose to his feet.

"No matter how well things are organized, there is always luck. Of all the staircases in the college Zinty and Krasner were allotted to M, to your staircase. Strange, isn't it?"

Junge turned away and looked towards the sea. Davie got up, flicked the sand off his trousers, and waited.

"I had meant to bathe again," said Junge. "But I don't feel very like it now. I think I'll go back to my hotel. If I may. If you mean what you say."

"I do mean it. I'm very glad to have had this chance of talking with you. There was one other thing. May I congratulate you on a splendid and beautiful book? You are Erich Kossuth, aren't you?"

"That book was anonymous, Dr. Davie."

"It was the publisher who told me it was by Erich Kossuth."

"If the author wanted to be anonymous the publisher ought not to have betrayed him. But my name, I assure you, my real name is Junge."

"It is now. But I think you were Kossuth to begin

with. Goodbye, Dr. Junge. I don't think somehow that we shall meet again."

"No, Dr. Davie. I don't think we shall. Please believe that I am grateful to you for all your kindness."

"Good swimming!" said Davie.

CAMBRIDGE

I

Davie had been dining at the Lodge on the night of his return from Italy; and at his request the Master had invited Cowl and Geoffrey Willow to join them.

"There certainly was a hoodoo on that conference," said Dr. Courtney. "Brauer, Zinty, Miss Banbury. And I see in the paper that Dr. Junge was drowned off Ischia somewhere. Was that while you were there?"

"Yes. I met him once on the beach and we had a long talk. He was one of those swimmers who try to reach the horizon. One day he didn't come back."

"Well, I hope that's the end of it."

"I hope so. I had a long conversation with Hodges today as soon as I got back. I think they really have reached the end of it."

"Do you mean it's solved?"

"Yes. It's solved."

"And they're arresting someone?"

"No—they aren't."

Davie paused. Dr. Courtney, Cowl and Geoffrey Willow looked at him. They didn't say "Why?" They waited.

"The police are entirely satisfied with the evidence," Davie went on. "But the person is dead. You can't charge someone who can't defend himself. This case will never come into court. It will never be proved or disproved. And so they can't name him."

"I bet you can," said Cowl.

"Yes," said Davie. "And that's why I asked the Master to invite you here tonight. The name can't be publicized. But it can't be hidden. Hodges agrees that I ought to tell you what I know."

II

"Looking back at it," said Davie half an hour later, "one can see that the solution really had its root in a rose petal."

"Ha!" said Cowl.

"I'm sorry to offend you," said Davie, "but I don't know how else to put it. There was no particular reason to insist that there had been a correspondence between Brauer and Stumpf. Indeed a man like Stumpf might well have preferred not to write letters. If I hadn't seen that rose petal and thought of the man with the red rose in his buttonhole I probably wouldn't have gone to see Mr. Stumpf. If I hadn't I wouldn't have identified Charlie. If I hadn't identified Charlie we wouldn't have got his evidence and it was his evidence that pin-pointed the timetable. Catherine couldn't know how soon after Brauer's fall Junge arrived at the conference office. But Charlie knew when he had left the Hall, and when he had seen them and they had seen him. Nobody else was around. It had to be Junge. But it took a long time to see it."

"Why did it *have* to be Junge?" asked Cowl after a long pause.

Davie smiled. "All right. I agree there was an alternative. But I couldn't take it seriously. There were moments, Geoffrey, when the evidence had a horrible tendency to point towards both you and Catherine. If I'd been a professional investigator I would have taken a powerful interest in you. It was only because

I knew you that I refused to include some things in my thoughts."

"What things?" said Cowl. "Perhaps he was an accessory before the fact. Have you thought of that? What things?"

"Catherine was outside the Hall. She'd have had plenty of time to jump off the scaffolding and get back to the office. And it was she who arranged the screens. Then Geoffrey knew Zinty in America. Geoffrey invited him to the conference. Geoffrey conducted him to his room and afterwards took Krasner there. He could have gone in and stayed to talk. But he didn't."

"I'm disappointed," said Cowl.

"It was Junge, waiting in the Dutch garden, who slipped in and joined them the moment Geoffrey had gone. It's a queer thing they had to be on my staircase."

"Not queer at all," said Willow. "I put them on M because I thought you'd keep a kindly eye on them."

"He did that," said Cowl. "As our pet and personal college investigator, you have done well, Davie. But I notice with regret that you have kept remarkably quiet on one or two rather important matters."

"Indeed yes," said the Master. "I remember, before you went away, you were extremely tiresome about the death of Miss Banbury. You seemed to imply that that presented no difficulties. Are you prepared to divulge?"

"Oh—yes—because I don't suppose the matter can ever be truly proved, and so my guess is as good as anyone else's. I told Hodges what I believed before I went away. He seemed to think it would serve. My theory springs from one morning, two or three days after Brauer's death, when I dropped my front stud, and wasted five minutes crawling about looking for it—till I suddenly remembered that studs sometimes amuse themselves by hiding in the turn-up of one's trousers. I looked and there it was. That evening, when I was changing a shirt before coming to dine here, I was going over all the mysteries of this case in my mind, and the mystery of Miss Banbury in particular. Why Miss Banbury? Quiet, good, totally harmless. What point could there be in killing her? None that I could see—and if none, then possibly the thing could have been a mistake. And as I thought about it I saw Miss Banbury as I had seen her on that last afternoon holding Brauer's head against her arm. Brauer was killed by a hypodermic needle. It should have been found. It wasn't. Now why shouldn't it have fallen, like my stud, into a bit of clothing? Miss Banbury was wearing a sort of knitted cardigan with pockets. Why shouldn't it have tumbled into one of those pockets? If it had done so there'd be nothing in the least remarkable in it lying there till Miss Banbury put her hand into her pocket on Tuesday morning, in an empty carriage, at the tail end of the nine o'clock train to Liverpool Street. And if it still contained poison that would be that. I don't know that that's the truth, but I think it's as near the truth as a guess is likely to be. The police have found nothing better."

"I'll award you a low mark for that, Davie," said Cowl. "A beta minus."

"Certainly," said the Master. "But what about all that stuff about the Combination Room door and the stolen blow-pipe? You were hot on those. I trust you're not going to say that you have been baffled by such trivialities?"

"No, I'm not, Master. I can explain both of them— and I'm afraid I've been keeping them to the last on purpose."

"Ah!" said Cowl. "The true artist. Proceed."

"I am sorry to tell you, Master," said Davie, "that your children are not truthful."

"Gracious! I know that."

"But children are bad liars. They contradicted themselves over the description of the man at the exhibition. At first I thought they were shielding someone. But when the stolen blow-pipe was found near the college—just outside your garden gate—with small smudged fingermarks on it, it occurred to me that the marks might have been made not by a man with small hands, and not by a woman, but by children."

"You don't mean—"

"Of course he does," said Cowl.

"There never was a man. It was the children who stole the blow-pipe and almost succeeded in leading everyone up the garden path."

"And how did you prove that, O ancient wizard?" asked the Master.

"By thinking about the mystery of the Combination Room door."

"Good title," murmured Cowl.

"I'd hurried down the Hall steps and into the cloister to get round to the dais via the Combination Room. It struck me afterwards that it was odd that I hadn't run into the person who'd been behind the screen and ought to have been escaping in the opposite direction at almost the same time. Then, ages after, I realized that I *had* run into him, almost, and hadn't realized it."

"I've no doubt you're enjoying yourself," said Cowl. "Spin it out, by all means. We are enthralled."

"Well—when I entered the cloisters I did see someone, through the arcading on the far side. But I hadn't accepted what I saw because it was only Richard, skipping along, waving what looked like a truncheon, but which I afterwards realized was the blow-pipe, and making for the cloister door to the Lodge. When I got back this afternoon I sought him out and told him straight that I believed he'd stolen the pipe. He admitted it at once. I think he was glad to have it off his mind. I asked him why on earth he'd done it—and what d'you think he said?"

"Don't ask me to think," said the Master. "Something ghastly of course."

"He said he wanted to see if it would fire a paper dart at Brauer during the lecture."

"Good Lord! Do you mean it was Richard who opened the Combination Room door?"

"Exactly so, Master. He did, and as he couldn't make the pipe work he sat down and pulled faces. I think Brauer's lecture would have been a failure anyhow. Richard is a boy of a very aspectabund countenance."

III

Later on, back in his rooms, Davie sat with a book on his knee, sipping Formosa Oolong mixed with jasmine. He looked over the top of his spectacles and smiled indulgently at the Boys Playing Marbles. He was already devoted to them, and to Letty, the Cow. Then he opened *The Last Will and Testament of Simon Cassidy*.

In the modern detective novel there is generally a paragraph on the page before the title page which recklessly discloses the early stages of the story as though in a desperate attempt to enlist the attention of an unwilling reader. From the sample before him it appeared that Simon Cassidy was a particularly nasty old man who had plainly injured at least six people, all of whom he had improbably invited to